RESCUED: MOTHER-TO-BE

BY
TRISH WYLIE

MILLS & BOON®

First published in Great Britain 2007
Harlequin Mills & Boon Limited,
Eton House, 18-24 Paradise Road, Richmond, Surrey TW9 1SR

© Trish Wylie 2007

ISBN-13: 978 0 263 19583 5
ISBN-10:   0 263 19583 X

CORK CITY LIBRARY	
06094451	
HJ	22/03/2007
	£12.25

Set in Times Roman 10½ on 12¼ pt
07-0207-50347

Printed and bound in Great Britain
by Antony Rowe Ltd, Chippenham, Wiltshire

Dear Reader

Do you remember *him*? You know who I mean; your first real crush, the guy who could make your heart beat faster just by smiling at you? We all had one in our teenage years, didn't we?

If we ever had the chance to see him again we'd want to look our best, to show him what he missed when he walked off into the sunset and broke our poor little hearts... Imagine, then, how Colleen feels when the one who broke her teenage heart walks back into her life looking better then he did before, more successful than he was before, while her life is a mess and she's the size of a small semi-detached house?

Thing is, when life throws you several curves, can you still have any faith in such a thing as happily ever after? In the magic that surrounded that first flush of love?

If you met *him* again, would *you* try?

I hope you'll enjoy Colleen's journey with Eamonn, a man who has spent half his life searching for something he left behind. And I hope that everyone who has as many curves thrown their way as Colleen has the chance to try again for that love of a lifetime.

But then, what can I say? I'm a romantic at heart, really...

Hugs & kisses
Trish

The music faded in the background, static sounded, and then the room surrendered to silence.

Colleen stayed focused on Eamonn's eyes, watching the movement of her hand on her stomach. It was one of the most intimate moments she had ever shared with a man, and yet it felt *almost right*.

Not as awkward as it should have felt, not as if they were crossing a boundary, and certainly not as if they'd spent the last fifteen years apart and were strangers.

Everything she was holding back from him faded into the background. For a brief, fleeting moment they were just two people caught up in the miracle of an unborn child. And Colleen knew she wouldn't forget the experience in a hurry.

Trish Wylie tried various careers before eventually fulfilling her dream of writing. Years spent working in the music industry, in promotions, and teaching little kids about ponies gave her plenty of opportunity to study life and the people around her. Which, in Trish's opinion, is a pretty good study course for writing! Living in Ireland, Trish balances her time between writing and horses. If you get to spend your days doing things you love, then she thinks that's not doing too badly. You can contact Trish at www.trishwylie.com

Trish spent her early childhood around horses in places similar to Inisfree in this book. To this day she works with Irish horses, both her own and freelance, as a show groom—when writing time allows, of course...

Trish also writes for Mills & Boon Modern Extra...

For Donna, Mary and Natasha,
who gave me enough information on pregnancy
to scare any sane single gal silly!

CHAPTER ONE

'WELCOME home, Eamonn.'

Colleen McKenna pinned a smile on her face and tilted her head back to look up at him where he stood, leaning against the doorway of the yard office. She had managed to keep her voice calm—even thought she'd come across as welcoming. Which was the least he deserved, on his first visit home after so long.

He hadn't changed a bit, had he? Still disgustingly good-looking, still able to dominate by sheer presence as much as size. And still, after fifteen years, capable of making her mouth go dry and butterflies flutter their wings erratically in her stomach. It really wasn't fair.

Surely a thirty-year-old woman should have long since been over the unrequited love she'd felt as a fifteen-year-old? Shouldn't she?

She felt a sudden ridiculous urge to raise her hand to her hair, to straighten it, tuck a loose strand behind one ear. As if those simple actions would somehow make her look less dishevelled than she felt. But it wasn't as if Eamonn Murphy had ever cared how she looked before, was it?

And it wasn't as if she could hope to measure up to the

breathtaking sight of him. Not while he was dressed in spotless walking boots, dark, low-slung jeans, and a thick chocolate-coloured sweater that hinted at the breadth of him as much as it hid.

He was glorious.

While Colleen knew she probably resembled a used teabag as much as she felt like one.

Hazel eyes, framed with thick dark lashes, pinned hers across the room, taking a brief moment to make an inventory of her face before a flicker of recognition arrived,

'Colleen McKenna.' A small smile lifted the edges of his sensually curved mouth. 'Well, you grew up, didn't you?'

'That happens, y'know. I could say the same thing about you.' She leaned back a little in the ancient office chair, the bulk of her body still obscured by the ridiculously large desk, and allowed her eyes to stray over his face. She swallowed to dampen her mouth. Oh-boy-oh-boy.

Had he got better-looking as he'd got older? She searched her memory to see if his hair had curled that way before, in an uncontrolled mass of dark curls that framed his face and touched his collar. Curls that invited fingers to thread through them, that looked as if that was exactly how they'd got that way in the first place. Yes. She remembered that. It had been a little of that irresistibly sensual edge which had been such a big part of him, and of his attraction.

She continued her mental checklist of his attributes, comparing old memories to the reality. Had he been as tall? Oh, yes, that she remembered. He'd always stood head and shoulders above every other boy she'd known, before and after he'd left. But the lean edge to him was gone, replaced by wide shoulders and a broad chest that made him seem even larger than she remembered.

It wasn't fair that he'd aged so well. But some people really did get better with age. Like good wine was supposed to. Not that there was enough in Colleen's weekly budget to cover the screw-top variety, never mind the kind that deserved being swirled around in a glass and savoured before drinking. Not that she was allowed alcohol presently. Not that she couldn't have used large quantities of it for self-medication these last few months.

Maybe just as well. If she'd started drinking to cover her problems she might not have stopped.

Eamonn dragged his eyes from her face and looked around the office, his eyes taking in the usual disorganised chaos. And inwardly Colleen squirmed.

It was stupid of her. It wasn't as if she hadn't known he would appear some time soon. But she maybe could have cleared up, filed things away, thrown a cloth over a surface or two. But all it really would have been was window dressing.

It wouldn't have helped to hide the awful truths she would have to tell him now that he was here.

But the least she could do was let him settle in first. There wasn't much point panicking about what had to come after that.

To hell with it.

When it came to the office he had to remember that paperwork was usually bottom of the chain around the place. He couldn't have forgotten everything?

It was plainly obvious *she* hadn't.

She cleared her throat and focused on less mundane matters. 'I'm sorry we couldn't hold off the funeral for you coming home. I really am, Eamonn. I know you'd have wanted to be here…'

Her voice died off into the silence and was eventually answered with a shrug of broad shoulders and in a husky deep voice. 'It's no one's fault, Colleen. You couldn't have got word to me where I was even if you'd known where to look. They didn't have phones there.'

Even with his easy dismissal she felt guilty. But what else could she say? She remembered only too well how people had struggled to say the right thing to *her* when her parents had died. It had been almost as awkward waiting for them to find what they considered to be the 'right words' as it had been for them to find them. And so many times she had wished they would just drop it, say what they had to in a card, or with a squeeze of her arm or even a hug.

But somehow she definitely didn't see herself offering a hug. An arm-squeeze was a possibility, *maybe*.

In the meantime, she picked up the conversation from what he'd said last. 'Another great adventure?'

'Something like that.'

She nodded. He was still a great talker, then. It was like getting blood from the proverbial—always had been. Just another thing that hadn't changed that much.

As a teenager he'd been dark and brooding ninety per cent of the time, and that had fulfilled all of Colleen's romantic notions. In her adolescent mind she had been going to be the one to tame him, to tease out his smile and put a spark in his eyes. She had even been encouraged by how he'd been in her company—how he had laughed, teased her, ruffled her hair. If he'd just once opened his eyes and noticed her the way she'd dreamed he would…

But she'd been a child and he'd been a mature eighteen-year-old, ready to leave the small hamlet they lived in to take on the world. And he'd left her behind.

Now, as he walked around the office, lifting breeding books and feed invoices and flicking them over, she knew she'd lived several lifetimes since then. She wasn't some doe-eyed teenager any more—wasn't a romantic dreamer. A kick or two in the teeth had that effect on a person over time.

He stopped and turned around, leaning back on one of the counters that were attached to three of the four walls and crossing his feet at the ankles before he folded his arms across his broad chest. 'I have to say I'm a bit surprised. The old place looks like hell. I take it Dad wasn't up to much the last few years?'

The American twang to his accent distracted her momentarily from his actual words. But when she caught them she automatically straightened her spine in her chair, words in defence of his father immediately jumping out of her mouth. 'Blaming it on Declan is hardly fair. He wasn't exactly fit for a lot of the heavy stuff after the second heart attack. You wouldn't even wonder about that if you'd seen him the way he was.'

Eamonn stared at her for a long moment, his gaze steady and impassive. 'This place was his pride and joy. It would have had to be something major to keep him from tending to it.'

'I'd say a couple of heart attacks *was* major, wouldn't you?'

There was a minute narrowing of his eyes. Then he blinked thick dark lashes at her. And said nothing.

Colleen suddenly felt like a bug under a microscope. It wasn't as if she had any right to criticise. All he had done was make an observation. But then, she knew inside that her defensiveness was less to do with Declan and more to do with her own part in the property's run-down appearance.

She pressed her lips together and released them with a small popping noise before taking a breath. 'Are you planning on staying long?'

'Depends.'

'Well, you'll be staying the night at least?'

'At least.'

Her blue eyes studied his impassive face for a few long seconds, and then she leaned forward again and smiled more genuinely. 'You were always hard work conversation-wise. I should have remembered that.'

One dark brow quirked at her candid statement, the corners of his sensual mouth twitching momentarily to hint at a single dimple on one cheek. 'Cut to the chase, don't you?'

'Well, I could play some kind of verbal game of chess with you, but I doubt I'd win. Life's too short for that sort of hard work, and I'm not really that smart. I like to try and believe people still mean what they say when they say it. Even when I still get reminded that's not always true. A girl can live in hope.'

'An optimist?'

She had to be. If she wasn't optimistic then there wouldn't be too much in her life to celebrate. 'I try to be. You only live the once—bit bloody pointless being depressed every day.'

His mouth quirked again.

Folding her slender arms across the top of the desk, she tilted forwards and bent her head to one side, her arched brows lifting in silent challenge.

Eamonn rewarded her with a burst of masculine laughter, the sound seeming to echo around the room. 'And to think you used to be shy.'

'I outgrew it.'

'Obviously. You outgrew a lot of things, from what I can see. And not too badly either.'

His eyes sparkled across at her, and for a moment her heart caught. *Ah, no.* He couldn't just waltz in looking all gorgeous and flirt with her. He was a decade and a half too late for that. *And* he had as much reliability as an ice cube on a summer's day.

Colleen had enough problems, *thank you.*

There was the sound of approaching hooves on the cobbled yard outside, and Eamonn's head turned towards the sound. He pushed off the counter and walked to the windows in a couple of long strides, looking out at each horse as it went by.

Tempting as it was to just sit and study his profile, all lit up from the window as it was, Colleen knew better than to let herself. So, her eyes on his curls, turning a dark chocolate in the sunlight, she pushed back from the desk and wandered across to stand a little behind him.

Her expert eyes glanced over each of the large animals as they walked by outside the window, taking in their conformation, their condition, the evenness of stride, assessing each one with an all-encompassing glance that took a matter of seconds. The rest of Inisfree Stud might look tatty round the edges, but the horses were still top class. It was the only point of pride she had left.

She glanced up at the side of his head. 'So, can you still not stand the sight of them?'

Eamonn turned his face towards hers and locked eyes once again, this time up close and personal. There wasn't the tiniest flicker in the hazel depths, or on his face. Not a hint of humour or regret. Just a simple blinking of his dark lashes as he took a moment or two longer than necessary to answer. 'Can't say I want to run out there and feed them carrots.'

So close to him for the first time in years, Colleen was suddenly overwhelmed by his masculine scent. In the company of horses most of the time, as she was, she wasn't used to such sensual tones. It was musky, spice with an underlying hint of sweetness, and it clung to her nose and pervaded her throat, almost as if she could taste him. And while she still had her head tilted up to look into his eyes the combination of awareness and proximity did things to her nerve-endings that hadn't been done for a long, long time. *If ever.*

It just wasn't fair. Someone somewhere really hated her, didn't they? Bringing him back *now*.

'My dad's biggest disappointment.'

The words caught her unawares, and for a split second she gaped up at him in open surprise. 'Eamonn, that wasn't your dad's biggest disappointment. Don't be daft. You couldn't force yourself to like them when you didn't.'

'I should have, though. It was in my genetic make-up.'

'Not everyone loves horses like—'

'Like *you* do?'

Colleen smiled then. 'I was going to say like your dad did. But I guess it's true of me too. It's just something that's in me.'

'Then you'll not understand how I feel any better than my dad did.'

Now, where had that come from? Why would he care what *she* thought? She was about to open her mouth and quiz him when he turned and, underestimating the space he needed to give her, brushed his arm against her stomach. Frowning, he dropped his gaze in surprise. Then his head shot back up, his eyes wide.

Colleen smiled ruefully. 'Don't worry—I bump things all the time now. It's not your fault. Just comes with the territory.'

'I didn't know.'

'No, well, it's not like I took an ad out in the paper in Outer Mongolia, or wherever it was you were.' She felt her cheeks warming, suddenly embarrassed by her condition. Well, at least under the scrutiny of someone she had once dreamed would have helped get her *into* that condition.

'Peru.'

'Peru, then.' She stepped back, her hand going to the small of her back as she made her way back to the desk.

'I didn't know you were married.'

'You don't have to actually *be* married to get one of these. I'm sure I have a book on high school biology somewhere you could read.'

Ignoring her sarcasm, he asked the obvious. 'So you're not married?'

'Nope.' She sat back down on the old chair, which creaked a little under her weight. 'Not married.'

'Engaged, then?'

She waved her hands in front of her face. 'Nope, no rings on these fingers.'

Not any more.

Eamonn looked surprised. 'You'll be *getting* engaged soon, though?'

Momentarily amused by his assumption, she shuffled the paperwork on her desk into a neater pile, and put it all back inside its manila folder. 'No. I tried that, and it didn't turn out so good. He walked. So there's just me and the fifteen-stone baby now.' She glanced up at him. 'I had no idea you were so old-fashioned.'

'Some things I'm old-fashioned about. Like a kid having two parents.'

'Well, this one will just have to make do with me.'

Eamonn stared at her in silence for a long, long time. Then, as if he couldn't help himself, he lowered his voice and asked, 'What happened?'

The question was an innocent one, she knew, and he meant well. Under normal circumstances she'd have been touched that he wanted to know. But he had no way of knowing how loaded a question it was—of the repercussions the answer would have on his own life. Or what those repercussions had meant for his father.

Colleen would never, ever forgive herself for the mistake she'd made. Because, thanks to her, Eamonn's father was dead. How exactly did she go about telling him something like that?

Looking into the hazel eyes that for most of her teenage years she had wanted to look at her with the kind of warmth they now held for a brief second, she just couldn't do it. She couldn't tell him. Not yet. Yes, she would have to at some stage. But just not yet. Not today.

'It ended badly.' Which barely began to explain what had happened.

'I'm sorry to hear that.'

Not half as sorry as Colleen was.

CHAPTER TWO

EAMONN didn't know what he'd expected when he'd come back to Killyduff, the tiny village he'd once called home. But if he'd had a list of things he *wouldn't* have expected…

Colleen McKenna being so grown-up had to be expected, he supposed. But she'd grown up pretty damn well. In his memory she'd been this scrawny little slip of a thing who had followed him around the farm like a puppy. She'd been a tomboy back then—sometimes in jeans, sometimes in riding jodhpurs, *always* in muddy boots. Wherever she'd been there had been a fat, hairy pony of some shape or other, and a dog with a permanently wagging tail. On the very odd occasion when she'd entered his thoughts that was how he'd thought of her. The little kid whose fair hair he had always ruffled.

She wasn't that now.

When he'd driven back through the narrow lanes and looked at the open scenery around him his mind had been filled with memories. So many of them bad ones—or happy ones tinged with a bittersweet after-taste. And when he'd walked into the office he had even been prepared for a moment to see his father behind the desk. Even though he'd known that wouldn't happen ever again.

Even though part of him had wanted the older man to be there. Just one last time. A ghost to lay to rest his own ghosts, or rather his demons.

The sight, then, of a fully grown, sparkling-eyed woman behind the desk his father had occupied for so long had caught him off guard. It had even taken him a few seconds to realise who she was. And then her direct way of speaking had amused him. The way her eyes would flicker away from him and then back had fascinated him.

But the sight of her so full and rounded with a baby? Looking as feminine as a woman could, lush and glowing. *That* had knocked him sideways.

Then to find out some jerk had walked off and left her like that…

Well, he wasn't sure why the thought of that annoyed him so much. Maybe simply because out of all the bad memories he had from this place he'd once called home it would have been nice to be left with one happy one. That the Colleen he remembered was happy and settled.

It would have been nice if *one* of them had figured out how to be happy.

If she'd been better settled he wouldn't have felt quite so bad about what he'd decided to do. He had hoped she'd be in a position to keep the place if she wanted to. But that wasn't looking likely, was it? It made him think somewhat more deeply about his plans.

What would she do when her baby came? How would she cope alone? How would she make her living? The questions shouldn't have been on his mind as much as they suddenly were. It wasn't really his concern, after all. But the questions were there regardless. And what had been planned as a flying visit—literally—wasn't looking so likely.

He took a deep breath. *Damn it.* It was a complication he didn't need. And it wasn't as if Colleen McKenna was *his* responsibility.

After a wander around the large old farmhouse, he threw some things out of his bag, showered, and searched through the cupboards for something to eat that might wake him up. Sleeping might be what his body craved, but he knew jet-lag well enough to know the sooner he adjusted to the time zone he was in the better.

Then, with the light fading outside, he wandered to the back of the house and looked out over the empty yard.

To catch sight of Colleen, pushing a huge wheelbarrow. *What the—?*

He was in front of the stable she was in in less than two minutes. 'What the hell do you think you're doing?'

Colleen's head jerked up at the sound of his sharp voice, and the huge grey horse beside her baulked. Immediately her hand came out, smoothing along the horse's wide neck to reassure it. 'Evening stables. What does it look like I'm doing? Belly dancing?'

Eamonn scowled as she smiled at her own joke. 'You shouldn't be doing this. Isn't there someone else?'

'The two girls we have left do most of it before they go home, but I do a wee skip round and check the rugs before I go to bed.'

'On your *own*?'

'Yes, on my own.' His astonishment seemed to surprise her. 'I'm pregnant, Eamonn. I'm not in a wheelchair. And keeping moving is good for me.'

'Wheeling a bloody great wheelbarrow about isn't.'

'Are you a gynaecologist now?'

'No, I don't need to be. It's common sense.' His eyes

narrowed as the large horse stepped towards him to investi-
gate. He shoved his hands into his jeans pockets and spread
his feet wider, as if preparing himself for an attack, which
made Colleen laugh aloud.

'I'd tell you Bob doesn't bite, but I'd be lying. And if you
keep your hands in your pockets like that he'll think you have
food.'

Eamonn removed his hands, held his palms out for the
horse to nuzzle in evidence of his lack of food, and tilted his
head to see past to what Colleen was doing.

She was lifting droppings onto a shavings fork. While he
opened his mouth to give out to her again, she spoke in a
softly firm voice. 'Bob, *back*.'

Bob dutifully stepped back from the door.

'And another one. *Back*.'

He stepped back again, leaving enough room for Colleen
to deposit what she was carrying into the wheelbarrow she
had placed across the open doorway. She looked around the
stable floor again. 'I'll be done in a minute anyway. I've just
this row to do.'

'I'm not happy with you pushing that wheelbarrow around
in your condition.'

'Thoughtful as that is, I've survived without your help this
far. I can make it to the end.'

'Are you always this stubborn?'

Her head turned as she fluffed the wood shavings into
place, one eyebrow quirking. 'I've always been this stubborn.
Don't you remember that much?'

'I remember you frequently being a pain in the—'

She laughed. 'Oh, I was that too.'

He wheeled the barrow out of the way as she came out of
the stable, pausing to pat the horse's neck again before she

closed the stable door, bolted the top bolt and kicked the bottom into place.

She then turned to retrieve the barrow. But Eamonn jerked his head towards the next stable. Stubborn only went so far with him. 'If I can't stop you then I'm wheeling the barrow. So hurry up.'

'I can do this just fine without your help.'

The rise of her chin and the glint in her eyes amused him, gave him a small sense of pride at her fierce independence that almost made him smile. *Almost.* If he smiled she'd think she'd won. And she hadn't. 'I believe you. But I'm here now, so learn to live with it. Now, hurry up. It's bloody freezing out here.'

'Warmer in Borneo, was it?'

'Peru. And, yes it was.' He jerked his head again, 'Go on, then.'

After a moment of hesitation, she sighed, and then moved to the next stable, where a finer darker head was over the door. 'Get back, Meg.'

Eamonn watched with less surprise as the animal did as it was bid. 'Do they all jump when you ask them to?'

'They know who's boss.'

He wheeled the barrow into place the same way she had at the previous stable, before leaning against the doorframe, watching her movements, and that of the horse, with cautious eyes. 'You're still taking a chance going in there, though. You know that.'

'Everyone who works with horses is taking a chance. It comes with the territory.'

Oh, he knew. Knew better than most people on the street. But then he'd seen first-hand what could go wrong, and that kind of memory tended to stick with a person. The day his mother had taken her bad fall he'd been ten. It had been the last time she had ever sat on a horse, and less than five years later she'd quit trying to like horses for her husband's sake. And left.

As the old memory seared across his mind and his heart, leaving a dull ache in its wake, he glanced around the empty yard. 'Don't any of the stable girls live in any more?'

'Not since the last foreign groom we had, no. They tend to live in the town. There's more going on there. The shops are closer—and, more importantly, the pubs.'

Eamonn put the pieces together. 'So you're out here doing this on your own with no one even within shouting distance?'

'Uh-huh.' She set her fingertips against the horse's side. 'Meg, *over*. Good girl.'

He was scowling by the time she dumped into the barrow again. 'So you're telling me you could get hurt and there would be no one here to help you 'til morning?'

'Pretty much.' She stopped, leaning on the handle of the shavings fork as she studied his scowling face in the dim light outside the stable. Then she shook her head and smiled. *'Jeez.'* She fumbled in her jacket pocket and produced a small mobile phone, which she wiggled back and forth in front of her. 'I can call for help. *See?* Prepared for every emergency, that's me. So you can quit fussing over me like an old mother hen. I'm grand.'

'Well, while I'm here you don't do this stuff alone.'

'What are you, now? My guardian angel?'

A brief nod in reply and, 'For now.'

The firmly spoken words made her eyes widen for a split second, and Eamonn felt a smile build on the corners of his mouth again. The kind of smile that made it all the way down inside his chest. When was the last time he'd smiled like that?

But then it *was* the first time since he'd come home that he'd felt vaguely in control. More like his usual self. And it was an even longer time since he'd had so capable a sparring partner. A victory was a victory, no matter how small.

Her blue eyes swept to a point above his head.

After a second he tilted his chin and looked upwards. Then he looked back at the deadpan expression on her face. 'What?'

'I think your halo's a little crooked.'

And just like that the victory was taken away from him. A burst of deep, resonating laughter escaped his lips. It had been one hell of a long time since anyone had spoken to him like she did. It was refreshing as be damned.

Colleen rewarded him with a glorious smile in return, 'Make yourself useful, then, and move the barrow. *Back*, Meg.'

The smile remained on his face as they made their way down the line of stables. Watching each horse from the corner of his eye, he observed how Colleen efficiently manoeuvred the animals, and did what she had to do with an ease of movement that spoke of confidence and physical ability, even with her ungainly size.

He allowed himself to study her closer.

She was very different from the women he'd known for most of his adult life. When he dated he dated in New York— his base for his travels. In New York he had the job that supported his many meanderings around the world in search of something he'd never found. In New York he filled in time between work and trips with the kind of women who dated professionally, who knew what face to present to the kind of guy they were trying to get. They dressed in clothes that accentuated their figures, had manicured nails, and hair that was tamed in such a way it was supposed to look natural. *But Colleen...*

Colleen was what Colleen was; there was no carefully constructed outer appearance. Her cheeks were flushed from the cold, and from the exertion involved in her task; her blonde hair was already escaping in long curling strands from the soft band that held it in a single ponytail at the nape of her neck. The long lashes that framed her startling blue eyes were free from mascara—as free as her full lips were from lipstick. In fact the redness of her lips was only due to how she would chew on them with the edge of her even white teeth as she concentrated on what she was doing.

And the rumour about pregnant women seeming to glow was apparently true too. All in all, she was the most naturally gorgeous woman he'd ever seen. And for the first time in his life Eamonn was finding a pregnant woman highly attractive.

What would be the point in that, though? It wasn't as if anything could come of it. His life was in New York, and the other places he journeyed to, and hers was in this tiny corner of Ireland he'd walked away from. With her horses. And it wasn't as if he spent a whole heap of time around kids—well, not every day anyway. A purely physical relationship was out of the question too. Because, apart from the most obvious restrictions, she was *Colleen*. She was practically family.

He was obviously a lot more tired than he'd thought. And he hadn't had a recent partner to distract him in a while. Something he would have to remedy when he got home.

Eamonn mulled it over as he pulled the barrow back from the door and moved to the next one.

Colleen was obviously a very capable woman. So what had him wheeling a barrow for her and offering to be her guardian angel? Being an angel wasn't something he was famous for, after all.

Maybe it was simply the age-old gene that demanded that the male of the species protect the female while she carried a child? A genetic thing in Colleen's make-up that made her attractive to him, so that he felt the need to *be* protective towards her?

He smiled at the thought. *Nah.* If that was all it was then he'd be chasing around after every vaguely pregnant woman, opening doors and offering to carry shopping. Though he guessed if he ever took a bus or a train anywhere he *would* give up his seat. But then he didn't need to take a bus or a train, he had a *driver*, and all it really proved was that he still had good manners.

It was more likely to be some kind of guilt.

And that thought made him frown. How could he hope to fix past wrongs by helping push a wheelbarrow around the yard now?

But, back amongst all the memories he had chosen not to remember about home, there had always been the hope that things would be better than he'd left them. That somewhere a simple form of happiness existed. Maybe by helping Colleen a little he could build that for her. Some.

At least before he pulled the rug out from under her feet. It certainly might make him feel better when he did.

'You'll give yourself a headache, y'know.'

He blinked as she stepped towards the door. 'I'll what?'

Colleen smiled a soft smile, her eyes twinkling in amusement. 'With all that thinking you're doing. You'll give yourself a headache.'

Eamonn found himself momentarily caught off guard again by her directness. When *was* the last time he'd been in the company of someone who said what they thought out loud at the drop of a hat?

Maybe it was a reflection of how far he'd gone in the world, of how successful he'd become. People no longer had that kind of honesty around him. And yet, if more people did, he'd probably have more respect for them. Like he did now, for Colleen.

There was a girlish giggle from the stable. 'Don't people have conversations in America?'

'Yeah, they do. But I guess I'm not used to someone being as blunt as you are.'

Colleen raised her chin and blinked a couple of times, a small line appearing between her arched eyebrows. 'Have you ever considered that that might be a reflection on *you*? You never were all that chatty, y'know. Puts people on edge—makes them careful about what they say.'

'I talk to people every day. It comes with the job.'

'And when's the last time you talked to someone about something that wasn't work-related?'

Good question.

She stepped towards the door, waiting for him to move the wheelbarrow as she absentmindedly stroked the horse's neck. And she spoke again, her voice lower. 'Yeah, that's what I thought.'

The barrow stayed still, keeping her prisoner inside the stable as Eamonn studied her intently. Then he shook his head. 'Don't you ever just think about things inside your head sometimes, without saying them out loud?'

Colleen went silent, something crossing over her face— something fleeting. But it had been there. Then as quickly as it had arrived it was gone, and she shrugged her shoulders. 'If I always say what I think then people don't have to try and read between the lines. There's less of a problem with inter- pretation. And that way mistakes are less likely to get made.'

Somehow Eamonn just knew there was a story behind that. But even as he phrased the question in his head she was pointing at the wheelbarrow. 'I thought you were helping?'

And the moment to ask her was gone as he moved the barricade. Maybe just because it was easier to let it go, not because he didn't *want* to know. He did. He was curious about her.

But curiosity wasn't really on the agenda. He wouldn't be there long enough, and it wouldn't matter when he left. Because he had no intention of ever coming back. There was nothing in Ireland that could hold him.

Though if Colleen hadn't been pregnant he supposed he might have stayed to play a while, to find out what was beneath her independent, capable façade. He was only human, after all. And he did like a challenge.

Maybe it was just as well she was pregnant. It put her out of reach. Kept her safe. Made things less complicated than they already were.

But the fact that he already liked what he had seen so far meant he would take the time to ease her into his plans. Out of respect, if nothing else.

He just needed to get some sleep first. So he was less distracted by her.

CHAPTER THREE

COLLEEN didn't sleep so well.

She could have blamed the baby entirely, but it seemed a tad unfair to be giving out to him or her before they even arrived. Her insomnia had as much to do with spending time around Eamonn as it did with a restless unborn baby.

Though the baby didn't help.

And the dreams her furtive imagination had conjured in the brief moments of sleep she had grabbed didn't help either. Her body was filled up with baby, for goodness' sake! It shouldn't feel the need to dream about the very act that had got it that way—even if in her dreams the players had been a tad different...

As she walked across the yard early the next morning she was smoothing her hand over her swollen stomach, trying hard to get what she thought was a bottom moved back into a more comfortable position, while she tried to focus her mind away from her dreams.

Babies were supposed to know how to get out, weren't they? If hers was unfortunate enough to have inherited his or her mother's sense of direction then it could well be pushing at her belly button so hard for the wrong reason. Not just because space was getting limited.

It was *very* uncomfortable. Almost painful.

But not anywhere near as painful as rounding the corner and finding Eamonn talking to the stable girls. They were giggling as she caught sight of them; one even had her hip tilted towards his tall frame. And for Colleen it was like a knife to the heart.

How many times had she walked around a corner or into a room or up to the school bus and found a girl looking at him like that? The answer was, quite honestly, dozens. And every single time it had killed her. Because he had smiled at them like he'd never smiled at her—laughed with them in a way he had never laughed with her. So that every single time she'd caught him flirting with them it had made her feel like a lesser person—because he didn't try to flirt with *her*. But this time it wasn't just a case of echoes of the jealousy she'd felt then, she reasoned, it had much more to do with a recent humiliation.

It wasn't Eamonn's fault, or the fault of the yard girls she knew so well. They weren't to blame for the sins of others. And Colleen scowled at her momentary weakness.

One of the girls caught sight of her scowling face and nudged the other as Eamonn turned in her direction. As the girls scampered off to work he moved towards her, and Colleen straightened her spine, pinning a smile in place.

It wasn't as if she had any reason to be jealous or angry. Not this time anyway.

'Morning.'

His voice was as soft as the smile he aimed her way, and she wished she had her old figure back so *she* could tilt her hip towards him as she spoke. For years after he'd left she had dreamed about him coming home to get her. Like some sort of a knight on a white charger.

Which had been a bit far-fetched, considering his lack of love for all things equine.

But in her fantasy she had been beautiful, ravishing, positively irresistible. Not blotchy, the size of a barn door, with swollen ankles.

Murphy's Law. She smiled at the irony.

'You look tired.'

Her smile faded. 'Flatterer.'

'I was just talking to the girls about them trying to do a bit more before they leave at night.'

Colleen blinked in confusion. 'A bit more? A bit more *how*, exactly?'

Eamonn shrugged. 'Just until your baby is here.'

The words stilled the hand on her stomach and she gaped at him. 'Why would you do that?'

'Why do you think?'

The blinking and gaping continued. Oh, this wasn't for real. Eamonn Murphy was looking out for her now? Taking her welfare on as his concern? Why would he do that? Was she so pathetic a figure?

'I've told you already, I'm not an invalid. And me and the girls have done just fine so far. I don't need you organising things for me.'

He fell into step beside her as she began to walk away, her head held high with a stubborn lift of her chin. Glancing at her profile with a small smile, he attempted to make peace. 'I'm *trying* to be helpful.'

'Well, you can knock it on the head.'

'I've had a look round the place this morning, and it seems to me you could do with some more help.'

The words stopped her dead in her tracks, as if she'd hit some invisible wall. Then she swung to face him, her eyes glinting in warning. 'And where were *you* when help was needed before, Mr Big-Shot?'

His smile faded instantaneously.

Even though guilt twisted inside her, Colleen couldn't have stopped the accusation from coming out. She shouldn't have said it, had no right to throw her own sense of guilt onto his shoulders, no matter how broad they were. And it wasn't as if his being there could have changed what had happened. But—

She swung a hand out to her side. 'While you were off wandering around Madagascar some of us were here, trying to keep this place going! *Some* of us felt this legacy was worth fighting for.'

The jibe hit home, and she watched as his nostrils flared and his eyes narrowed for a very brief second. Then he stepped in as close as her distended belly would allow and leaned his head in closer, his voice low. 'I've never been to Madagascar. And if I'd had any idea this place was in such a bad state I'd have done something about it before now. You think if Dad had even once told me he needed help that he wouldn't have got it? I knew what this place meant to him, Colleen. And I could have done something to fix it if he'd told me.'

Even while the voice of reason shouted in her head for her to shut up, she was raising her chin again, so she could look him in the eye rather than focus on the sensual sweep of his mouth. If she focused on his eyes she could try to ignore the wild beating of her pulse in response to his proximity. She could pretend that she had control over the rapid thud of her heart. She could give herself a moment to control her breathing.

But looking into his eyes so close up wasn't any less distracting. Up close she could see that there were flecks of gold through the hazel—gold that seemed to glow fiercely at her as he stared her down. And anger rose up in her stomach in reaction to her own lack of self-control.

'Your father and mine built this place out of love. You throwing money at it wouldn't be the same thing. There's no way in hell your father would have taken your money, and you know it. It wasn't *money* he needed from you!'

The gold flared. 'Money would have let him keep this place the way he wanted it. And we both know this place meant more to him than anything else, don't we?' He smiled sarcastically. 'The world doesn't revolve around love.'

Colleen's breath caught. Fighting down a wave of hurt, she answered him with a tight-lipped, 'Oh, I *know* that. I know that better than most people, *thanks*.'

One large hand caught her arm as she turned away. Held it tight in a vice-like grip for a second, before she looked down at it, and then back up with a determined gaze. A gaze that said clearly, *Back off or I'll fight you off.*

Unexpectedly the hold softened, his thumb brushing back and forth as his voice sounded in a low grumble. 'Is it really so hard for you to let someone look out for your welfare? Even for a little while?'

Her heart thundered loud in her chest, and she took several breaths to calm herself while she freed her arm with a small twisting movement. Looking down again, she rubbed at the heated place where he had touched, as if rubbing it would somehow remove the brand of his touch. 'You won't be here that long, Eamonn. There's no point in me getting used to you looking out for me.'

Eamonn stood statue-still as her eyes slowly rose to meet his.

She forced a tight smile into place. 'I'm a big girl. I can look out for myself. It's not that I don't appreciate what you're doing. But, really, there's no need. We horsey women are made of sterner stuff.'

He didn't move as she turned away from him. But in the

space of a heartbeat—less time than it took for her to retreat two steps—his deep voice sounded again. 'Fight me all you want, Colleen McKenna. But you're getting my help.'

Colleen stopped dead—didn't look at him, couldn't, her heart still beating loud in her chest. It didn't make any sense. What did it matter to *him*?

'Why?' It was as eloquent a reply as she could manage.

'Because it's fairly obvious you need it, whether you'll admit it or not.' He moved closer to her with one long step, his voice sounding above her ear. 'Put it down to a guy thing, if you have to. But that's the way it is. You won't change my mind.'

There was a brief pause. Then he continued. 'I found your stuff in the house this morning. You've been living there, rather than in the Gatehouse. So where did you stay last night while you avoided me?'

Colleen felt her cheeks flame. She hadn't been back to the Gatehouse since her world had fallen apart. But telling him that would be opening up a can of worms, and she still wasn't ready. 'The Gatehouse is kept for renting out. And it's rented now, as it happens. I slept in one of the rooms above the stables.'

'Why?'

'Because technically it's your house now.' She aimed a glance over her shoulder. 'It didn't feel right, that's all. I wasn't avoiding you. I was respecting your space.'

A small exhalation of breath accompanied by a quirk of his dark brows told her he wasn't buying that. Then his eyes skimmed over her face as he spoke. 'Well, I'd prefer it if you stayed in the house. It's been your home for a while, judging by how much of your stuff is there.'

'Your dad started to find it tough getting around. It made sense to have someone keep him company. In case he needed help with anything.'

Eamonn's face darkened. 'I didn't know he was that bad.'

'No.' With a sigh, she turned and lifted her chin to look up into his face. 'And that wasn't your fault—not entirely. He wouldn't have told you, was too proud to ask for your help. He was a stubborn man.'

He glanced down for a moment, his thick lashes disguising his thoughts from her. Then he took a breath and lifted his chin, looking deeply into her eyes for a long, long moment. Almost as if he was searching for something. 'Then maybe he and I weren't all that different after all.' Another breath, and he added, 'You'll stay in the house, Colleen, whether it's mine or not. And you'll accept my help 'til this baby is born. No arguments. That's the way it's going to be, and that's that.'

She opened her mouth to argue.

But he spoke again. 'I may not have been here to help him when I should have. But I'm here now. You're getting my help, so learn to deal with it.'

Colleen stood in the middle of the cobbled yard as he walked away, his long, confident strides putting distance between them. And even while her mind recognised that the baby had shifted into a position where it wasn't so painful, she was deeply aware of another ache. In her chest.

Eamonn might be righting some of his perceived past wrongs by helping her out. Wrongs that might be monumental in his mind, but could be nothing compared to what *she'd* let happen. Maybe he remembered as much about the day he'd left as she did—the words that father and son had thrown at each other in the heat of the moment. But he hadn't been responsible for the man's death.

While Colleen had. Indirectly.

She had no right to accept any form of a helping hand

from Eamonn. No matter how much she might want it. And no matter how much she would reluctantly admit to herself she could do with it.

Regardless of all that, even under perfect circumstances, there would be no point in becoming reliant on him. Because he wouldn't stay. It wasn't in him. Never had been.

No matter how much the young Colleen might have wanted to be taken care of by him, how she had longed for him to simply care, the simple fact was he never had.

And if he hadn't ever looked at her back then, there was just no way in hell he would look at her now she was damaged goods. Even before he knew everything.

No, Inisfree was the only thing she had left. The fact that it was in such a mess, that she couldn't afford extra staff to do the work even temporarily, 'til she had her baby, was her fault at the end of the day. The burden was hers alone.

And the sooner Eamonn went back to his glamorous world the better. Because she couldn't let herself get sucked back into a useless fantasy.

But knowing all that didn't stop her chest from aching as she stood alone in the centre of the yard, watching him walk away.

CHAPTER FOUR

'How long will you be there, do you think?'

Eamonn pressed the phone between his ear and his shoulder as he worked on his laptop, and his partner's voice continued. 'Gimme a vague idea.'

'I really don't know, Pete. It's more complicated than I thought it would be.'

'Well, I won't say I couldn't do with you here. Marcy is making me crazy with all the extra hours I'm doing. I could be divorced by the time you get back.'

Eamonn smiled. 'Nah, I doubt that, somehow. Though why she married you in the first place is still a mystery to me. She's too good for the likes of you.'

'That's as may be. But now that she's got me, I'd kinda like it if she hung on. At least when your workaholic butt was here she got to see me.'

'It's about time you did something, right enough. I couldn't keep carrying the both of us for ever.'

Laughter sounded down the line. It wasn't true, and they both knew it. Eamonn had struck gold when he'd met Pete. Fourth generation Irish, the gentle giant had taken the newly arrived, wet behind the ears Eamonn under his wing in the big city. Without his help and his contacts Eamonn might never have made it. And he would never forget that.

'You couldn't carry me if you had a truck.'

Eamonn smiled. 'I have the info here on the Queens project. I'll look it over and e-mail you back any thoughts I have—okay?'

'No problem, buddy.' There was a pause, then, 'You doin' okay?'

'Course I am.' But even as the words came out he was asking himself if they weren't a lie. He didn't know *what* he was.

'Can't be easy, missin' your dad's funeral and all.'

Eamonn took a breath, moved the receiver from one ear to the other. No, that part wasn't easy. The least he could have done was be there to pay his respects. To say sorry for not having come back sooner. He'd always thought there would be time—that the bridges that had started to mend through phone calls would be the first steps towards him seeing his father again face to face. Instead he'd had to make do with a silent vigil by a graveside under a grey sky that had wept tears he couldn't shed himself. Weeks after his father had been buried. It didn't make him feel like much of a man.

'I have a couple of issues to work through. But I'm fine, Pete. Really. You don't need to worry.'

'Well, look, I hope the visit home does you good. You've been restless a while now.'

Wasn't that the truth? He'd tried burying himself in work for years, had made a clean fortune out of it. But that hadn't been enough. He'd dated—stunningly beautiful women, as it happened—but nothing that had lasted. And he'd travelled, seen parts of the world he could only have dreamed of when he'd been growing up in the wilds of Ireland.

But he was still restless.

And now he was rearranging his life to continue a visit that should have taken only a few days, to take care of someone who really didn't want his help.

He took another breath. 'I'll send this stuff through in a while, Pete. E-mail me anything else that comes up, and we'll work that way 'til I get back.'

Pete took a similar breath and gave up. 'Right. Okay, then. I'll talk to you soon.'

'Send my love to Marcy.'

'Sure I will. *If* I ever get to see her again.'

Eamonn set the receiver down and stared at the laptop screen for a long while, his eyes not even focusing on the e-mail. *What was he doing?*

The next time he saw Colleen he was going to have to have more belief in her strength and tell her why he'd come back. What it was he wanted to do to sever his ties for good.

It just would have been easier if she'd been in a position to buy him out. If he hadn't thought that telling her his plans might be the one thing to break the thin hold she had on what she obviously cared about the most. The thing he needed gone, so his last link to Ireland was severed. And he'd never have to come back again.

It was just business. That was all.

Colleen avoided him for as long as she could. But eventually the growling in her stomach refused to be ignored. And though on her own she could have coped with hunger, she wasn't eating just for herself. As if somehow sensing she was being stubborn about it, the baby leaned on her again. *Hard.*

She smoothed a hand against the protruding bump. 'All right, I hear you. We'll go now.'

Eamonn was already in the large old kitchen when she came in through the door, his laptop open on the huge wooden table.

He glanced up at her, his eyes studying her face for a long moment. 'You feeling okay?'

Colleen quirked a brow. 'Are you going to ask me that every time you see me?'

His mouth twitched, eyes sparking. She was just so defensive sometimes, so determined to challenge him, that it amused him. How else was a man supposed to react to a woman so gloriously large with child? It was his *job* to be considerate, even if he wasn't the father. That was what the good guys did.

What amused him more was that being around her had him thinking of himself as a good guy. Being a bad boy around women had always worked for him better.

She tilted her head and continued. 'I have to go to the toilet the second I finish a cup of tea, my back aches, but not as much as my feet, and the baby has been trying to push a hole through my stomach all day. But apart from that I'm just grand. Is that enough information for you, or should I go into a bit more graphic detail?'

A low whistle sounded between his teeth. 'Man, but you're testy, aren't you?'

'*Testy?*' She blinked at the word. 'As soon as nature organises it for men to carry the babies you can talk to me about being testy.'

'The human race would die out.'

'You're damn right it would.'

When he grinned, a dimple appearing in full glory on his cheek, she smiled back. It was a rare flash of acquiescence. But she couldn't hold his gaze for long, though, and felt a flush building on her neck. Instead she nodded at the fridge. 'I came to get something to eat. Have you had lunch?'

'No, I haven't.' It wasn't a big surprise. He'd always been one of those people who could get through from breakfast to dinner so long as there was coffee. But he was irritated he hadn't thought of Colleen. So much for being a good guy.

He pushed his chair back from the table, the legs screeching on the slate floor. 'Sit down. I'll rustle something up for us.'

Colleen shook her head, reaching a hand up self-consciously to tuck a long curl behind her ear. 'You're doing it again. I can make a sandwich—thanks anyway.'

Glancing at her with a spark of warning in his eyes, he pointed a long finger at the table. *'Sit.'*

With no idea why she did it, she sat down as she was bid. But she eased her annoyance with herself for obeying by pouting. And then felt childish. *Damn him.*

'Is there anything you can't eat?'

She folded her arms defensively across her breasts. 'Is that a dig at my size?'

There was brief moment of tense silence, and then he laughed at her deadpan expression, the oh-so-male sound echoing around the cavernous room. 'No-o. It was a query in case anything I made would make you sick.'

Her mouth pursed momentarily in thought, before she sighed dramatically. 'Not really. I've been past all that stuff for a while. But if you put a pickled anything in it, it would taste one heck of a lot better.'

Inside a few minutes he had made sandwiches, with pickled onions on one side of hers, and two steaming mugs of tea. To distract herself from watching him move around the kitchen, Colleen allowed herself to glance at his laptop screen. *It* had no effect on her pulse whatsoever.

He pulled up a chair beside her. 'It's work.'

Flushing slightly at having been caught looking at what could have been private information, she avoided his gaze. 'No rest for the wicked, eh?'

'Apparently not. In which case I must have been *really* bad at some point.'

Concentrating on her sandwich for a moment, while her mind did outrageous translations of '*really* bad', she then risked a sideways glance at his face as she raised the sandwich to her lips. 'Sharon Delaney being a good example, I suppose?'

Eamonn's eyes widened a fraction. 'You knew about that?'

'Half the village knew about it.'

'Nothing actually happened.' There was no reason for him to explain that to her, but he continued. 'Staying out all night got us in enough trouble.'

'Oh, I *remember.*'

Eamonn's attention was drawn from the teasing light in her blue eyes to her mouth as she bit into the sandwich. He watched her lips close around it, watched as she licked bread-crumbs away with the tip of her pink tongue. It was one of the most sensual things he'd ever witnessed. Who knew that a sandwich could have such an effect? It never had before that he could recall.

'What else do you remember?'

Colleen turned her face away from his intensive gaze, her voice dropping. 'I have the memory of an elephant.' She smiled. 'Size of one at the minute too.'

'You keep on doing that. You're not all that big. You're having a baby, and that's one of the most amazing things a woman can do.'

The softly spoken words touched a chord in her heart. She

looked over at him, but he had turned his face away, leaving only his profile to her inquisitive gaze as he bit into his own sandwich.

It was one of the nicest things anyone had said to her of late. And at a time when she could stand a compliment or two. Waddling around every day certainly didn't make her *feel* amazing.

But her guilt was still present, and she just didn't know how to answer him because of it. She didn't deserve compliments from him.

While she thought, Eamonn was doing some thinking of his own. Without changing position, he stared straight ahead and asked, 'How long since he left?'

In a split second the warm glow from his words disappeared and was replaced by an icy chill. 'Six months.'

Out of his peripheral vision he saw her head bow, her attention back on her food. So he turned his face towards her and watched the slow flutter of her long lashes against her cheeks. 'What happened?'

Setting her sandwich back on the plate, she reached for the warmth of her mug, wrapping cold fingers around it. 'He left with one of the stable girls. They'd been carrying on for a while.'

Eamonn might be many things, but slow wasn't one of them. Maybe that was part of the reason she'd been so defensive earlier, when he'd been talking to the girls? It had brought back bad memories for her. But he let it go. *One step at a time, Eamonn.* Pushing Colleen didn't always have the desired result, after all.

'You had no idea it was going on?'

'I think I knew, deep down. But I'm stubborn, remember? I thought it would all work itself out.' She spoke over the rim of the cup, shrugging her shoulders. 'He could be very charming, and I think a part of me was swept off my feet by him. At least at the start. So I could hardly blame some naïve girl for falling for him.'

She touched her mouth to the mug, hesitated, and glanced briefly at Eamonn's face. 'We see what we want to see sometimes, I guess.'

'Did he know you were pregnant?'

'Yes. No man who's about to be a father shouldn't know, don't you think?'

Eamonn tilted his head and nodded briefly as she sipped out of her mug. 'I'd want to know if you were having my baby.'

Colleen almost choked on her tea, her eyes watering as she forced it to go down the right channel without too much fuss. *Dear Lord.* Had he any idea what that statement did to a mind already full of night-time images? If he'd said something like that to her when she'd carried all those unrequited dreams before…

'But then if it was mine I would never have left.'

Oh, c'mon! Her eyes widened at the statement as she turned to look at him. Why did he have to say things like that? Why did the words just have to roll off his tongue as if he was discussing the weather? Had he really no idea of the dreams she'd had as a teenager? Had he no idea at all that hearing parts of them spoken aloud now was like a kick in the teeth to a woman who had so seriously managed to pick the wrong man to be father to her child?

When she found words, they were almost a plea for him to understand how ridiculous his own words had been. 'Right—that's what you'd do. Even if it meant staying in a place where you hated being. That makes a lot of sense.'

'I didn't hate it here.'

She made a small snort of disbelief.

But his voice remained steady. 'I just didn't feel like I fitted in, and I was young—I thought there was more to life. That I should have a go at finding out.'

'And was there?'

There was a brief electric pause as he looked her in the eye. Then he shrugged. 'I've made more money in the States than I would ever have done here, that's for sure.'

'And is that enough? Are you happy, Eamonn?'

The sound of his name in such a soft tone caught him. Without thinking, he brought his gaze back to her mouth, and he stared for a long moment, mesmerised, before forcing himself to look up. He blinked—once, twice. Then, still not thinking it through, he reached a finger out and tucked the ever-errant strand of hair behind her ear again, before pushing his chair back, his voice low. 'I'm not so sure it *is* enough.'

Looking down at her stunned expression, he smiled wryly. 'And, just for the record, that's the first time I've said that out loud.'

CHAPTER FIVE

A GROWN, mature woman, in charge of her faculties really shouldn't feel shyness. But it was like being fifteen all over again when she ventured into the house after dark.

All afternoon—while she'd made phone calls, arranged for vet visits, ordered wormers and checked feed store levels—her mind had been obsessed by one fleeting touch and a softly spoken confession.

Which had led her to ask several silent questions. The main one being: what had happened to him since he'd left?

Surely someone who looked the way he did hadn't been lonely? At least not for long. Colleen remembered vividly how girls had gravitated towards him. She'd hated every single one of them back in the day.

And yet the look on his face when he'd spoken had reflected a deep sense of loneliness, almost of need. The part of her that had cared so much for him so many years ago desperately wanted to understand why. Not that there was anything she could do to help beyond listening—if he would deign to talk.

It was a complication she could have done without. One that held her own confession back when it really should be something she got out into the open. Sooner rather than later. Avoiding it just made it worse.

As she kicked off her boots at the back door an unfamiliar noise greeted her ears. And as she worked her way through the kitchen and along the hall it got louder, positively deafening by the time she reached the family room at the front of the house.

When she peeked around the half-open door she couldn't help but smile.

Eamonn's head was nodding up and down in time to the music, his hand absentmindedly playing an air guitar with one hand as he looked through the dusty box in front of him with the other.

And then his voice sounded, loud and distinctly off-key, as he joined in with the music.

Colleen hid her mouth behind her hand and giggled. She couldn't help herself.

But he obviously hadn't heard her. He shook his head again, the curls on his dark cap of hair shifting, and then he raised both hands above the box and drummed in time with the bass beat.

With her hand still covering her mouth she let her eyes move over him from her position of safety. From the shifting curls, down past his wide shoulders to his tapering waist and the rounded curve of his behind. And deep inside of herself a mischievous imp prayed he would wiggle it. Just the once. *Please*.

Of course he chose that moment to turn and look directly at her.

Her eyes shot up and met his.

Slowly, ever so slowly, his hands lowered to his sides, and he smiled a little ruefully before moving over to the old record player and turning down the volume.

After a brief clearing of his throat, his deep voice rumbled in the sudden quiet. 'I found some of my old collection up in my room.'

She plucked up her courage and walked into the room. 'So I heard. Nice singing, by the way.'

His shoulders shook briefly in silent laughter. 'Never did have much of a singing voice.'

Moving around the end of the sofa, Colleen eased down onto the well-worn cushions, lifting her aching feet onto a generously stuffed footstool. Then she sighed contentedly as she slid down into a comfortable position, her stomach rising before her eyes.

She blinked a couple of times at the sight, still sometimes finding it hard to equate the sight of the bump with her own body.

Eamonn replaced the rock music with a softer track as he watched Colleen smooth her hand over her stomach from the corner of his eye. She did that a lot during the day, he'd noticed. With only a moment of hesitation he stepped over her feet and sat down beside her, his head tilting to rest on the sofa-back.

And they sat that way for a long time as the record played, static sounding between tracks.

It occurred to Eamonn that it was the longest time he'd ever spent completely silent in a woman's company. And it wasn't an entirely unpleasant experience.

Then, with a turn of his head in her direction, he caught sight of her poking her fingers against an irregular bump below her crimson shirt. Her fingers circled it, pushed a little, circled again. When he looked up at her face she had her eyes closed. But she was smiling a small, secretive smile.

His gaze back on her fingers, he asked in a low voice, 'Is that a foot you're pushing?'

'I think so.' She opened her eyes, tilted her head forwards, so that her chin rested on her chest, and looked down at her hand, smoothing the soft material around the small bump so it was more defined.

'Doesn't it hurt when that happens?'

Long lashes fluttered as she raised her eyes to his, surprised by the look of fascination she saw there. 'Not as much as when the precious pushes its bottom out. That can be *very* uncomfortable.'

The golden flecks in his hazel eyes glowed warmly across at her. 'Does he do that often?'

Colleen smiled an amused smile. *'He?* What makes you so sure the baby is a he?'

'She, then?' The corners of his mouth twitched, hinting at a smile being held inside. He did that a lot, she'd noticed. As if he always felt the need to keep himself in check, controlled. It made her ache to tease the smile out, to have him soften and relax when he was around her.

Her smile grew in return. 'Haven't the faintest. I'm a leave-the-presents-'til-Christmas-morning kind of girl.'

The music faded in the background, more static sounded, and then the room surrendered to silence as Colleen stayed focused on Eamonn's eyes, watching the movement of her hand on her stomach. It was one of the most intimate moments she had ever shared with a man, and yet it felt *almost right*. Not as awkward as it should have felt, not as if they were crossing a boundary, and certainly not as if they'd spent the last fifteen years apart and were strangers.

Everything she was holding back from him faded into the background. For a brief, fleeting moment they were just two people caught up in the miracle of an unborn child. And Colleen knew she wouldn't forget the experience in a hurry.

Didn't want to. What she wanted was to savour it, to hold on to it like a security blanket for later reference, when she would be alone again. Because moments like this one were what she should have had. It was a sense of togetherness, of companionship, which she had been denied by the one person who should naturally have shared the experience.

His lashes brushed his tanned skin as he blinked. 'Are you scared, Colleen? About having a baby?'

Her heart thundered at the husky question. She looked away from his face and down to where his hand rested over his lap, focusing on his long tapered fingers, on his neatly cut clean nails. 'I guess I am. I don't know who wouldn't be. It's natural to feel that way. I just hate that I am, so I try to ignore it.'

His chin rose as she made the confession. He waited, hoping she would lift her eyes so he could look into their blue depths while she spoke. So he could try and see behind her words and into her mind. It occurred to him that maybe, just maybe, she hid behind her brave words and smart mouth.

But although her head moved it was away from him, her eyes focusing on her stomach as she continued. 'Some days it doesn't feel real. Like I'm not actually going to have this little life that I'm totally responsible for. That'll become the centre of mine.'

Her breasts rose and fell as she took a breath, drawing his eyes in that direction. He stared, mesmerised by the simple sensuality of the movement.

Her soft voice sounded beside him. 'And you can con yourself into believing that at the start.' Her mouth twitched. 'When your body hasn't changed and you haven't put on too much weight. Until the first time the baby moves and you realise it's really happening. Then it hits you. And I just— Well, I worry. I worry that I might not be able to give this baby everything it needs, be a good enough parent.' She paused. 'Does that make any sense?'

He managed to raise his gaze as she turned her face to his. But when her eyes flickered to his in question he froze, the air trapped in his chest. The answer was suddenly terribly important to him.

It wasn't something he'd ever had to think about. He was man, after all. Yes, somewhere in the back of his mind he'd maybe always believed that he'd have kids of his own some day. But he'd never actually put a specific date on it happening, or thought about the woman who would carry his child. It had been a long way ahead; it hadn't involved planning, or thinking how he'd feel when the time came.

Hadn't *ever* involved thinking about how the woman might feel in that situation. How frightening it must be for her first time out. Let alone doing it without any support from a partner or family.

But now, sitting beside Colleen while she told him how she felt, it *made* him think. And he knew he would worry too, if it were happening to him, if a child of his was so close to coming into the world and changing his life for ever. It would be scary as all hell. Could he be a great dad when the time came? The kind of father a child deserved?

Could he be a better father than he'd been a son?

With no firm answers to his silent questions he knew one thing. *He'd try.*

With his eyes fixed on hers, he simply nodded, and she bestowed a shimmering smile on him in reply. But even as he found himself smiling back without reservation she turned her face away from him, hiding her expression before she surprised him again by confiding, 'This isn't the way I pictured it being in my head. I always thought I'd have the whole package—husband, happy home, that kind of thing. And it's not that I'd change things the way they are right this minute—not completely, anyway. I just worry that I might not be enough on my own.'

'You're not on your own.' Eamonn found himself reaching out for the hand that rested on the tiny foot, her fingers stilling as he tangled them with his. *'I'm* here.'

The baby pushed up against their joined fingers and he stared, transfixed at the sheer magic of it. Magic of a kind he'd never experienced. Warming his soul.

But Colleen broke the spell, her body stiffening as she pulled her hand free from his, her voice low and matter-of-fact as she turned her face to his again. 'I can't learn to rely on that, though, can I? It's not like you're here for long. You have a life of your own. I'll get through, don't worry. It's what I do.'

Eamonn remained silent as she pushed herself up onto her feet. He should have had an answer for her—something to reassure her that he would be there to help. But she was right, wasn't she? He *couldn't* be relied upon to stay.

She stopped at the doorway and smiled again. A different kind of smile, more cautious. 'Soon you'll be gone, and life will go on like it did before. I guess, whether I'm enough for this baby or not, I'm just going to have to try to be. That's just the way it is. We'll be fine.'

Outside the room, Colleen stood and stared at the banister for a long while.

When had she got so lonely?

Because she had to be, didn't she? To sit and spill her guts to someone who had been out of her life for so long? Who, when he left this time, would probably be gone for ever. There would be nothing to bring him back after all.

With a deep breath she allowed that *that* was maybe why

she'd just spilled her guts. She could talk to him, share some of her deepest-held fears, within the safety net of knowing there could be no repercussions.

Knowing that he would never bring her deepest fears into a future argument in the knowledge that hitting her insecurities was the surest way to cause her pain.

That made him safe.

The thing was, for a brief moment, in the warmth of that room, while soft music played and shared intimacy warmed her heart, it had been easy to trust. Just for a moment.

Until he had taken her hand and her baby had moved in response. Then she had felt the gaping hole inside her chest—felt the future loss of something she didn't even have from him in the first place.

For not the first time in six months Colleen felt tears well in her eyes. God, how had she made this big a mess? How had her life ended up like this?

And how could she keep on holding everything together when being around Eamonn made her feel so bloody vulnerable?

With an angry swipe of her hands against her cheeks she lifted her foot onto the first stair. Then, raising her chin as she ascended, she searched even deeper into the rapidly diminishing well of her inner strength.

Why couldn't he just leave, already?

And why couldn't she just quit stalling and tell him what he had a right to hear? That would be enough to send him packing!

Maybe that was just it. The part of her that was holding back was the part of her that didn't want him to leave. The same part that hadn't wanted him to leave the first time round.

The part that should have already learned its lesson. Because Eamonn Murphy wasn't a happily ever after. Not for her.

CHAPTER SIX

I'M HERE. You're not on your own.

Eamonn spent half the night wondering why on earth he'd felt the need to say that to her. It wasn't as if he planned on staying beyond a couple of weeks—which was already a couple of weeks more than he'd intended originally. Fly in, sort out what he had to sort out, and fly out. It was business, that was all.

And then he would be back to his own life. Back to the place where he had work and a swish apartment and friends. Back to six months of hard slog before the familiar restlessness would set in…

And yet all it had taken was fifteen or twenty minutes in a warm room, witness to a small miracle in evidence of a new life, and he was suddenly volunteering to stick around.

What was *with* that?

After a restless night he decided to tend to more practical details. Some good old-fashioned physical labour would put paid to thinking in circles. And to obsessing about the feel of Colleen's hand in his, the sight of her breasts as they rose and fell. Yep, lots of physical labour was called for.

So, with early-morning yards already starting outside, he

pulled on the closest thing he had brought to practical working clothes and went to inspect the property. After all, it made sense to give it a bit of a tidy-up. It would increase its value.

But inside an hour he was scowling. Hard. The place just shouted neglect—and that wasn't how he remembered it. When he'd lived here every fence had been neat and well maintained, all the pastures had lain in smooth, weed-free paddocks, gates had swung open with the push of a hand. Now there were broken railings, tall weeds in patches, gates tied with pieces of rope that had to be lifted to get through them.

It made him unreasonably angry.

Because all of it yelled lack of money. Why couldn't his father have asked for help? Inisfree had meant so much to him. And why hadn't Eamonn ever taken the time to swallow his own damn pride and come home to visit? Then he would have seen the decay with his own eyes. He could have fixed it!

For half of his life he had worked hard to be a success, and maybe during that time he should have called more, written more, visited more. But he'd been so driven to make a success of himself, to prove himself. Maybe even to impress Declan Murphy.

If he hadn't managed to grant his father's deepest wish, to stay and love Inisfree like he had, then he *had* to be a success at something else. But, in the end, was his very success the one thing that had stopped Declan from admitting his own failure? Had the father/son relationship disintegrated to that low a level?

Would giving his father money to help out have made Eamonn feel any less guilty? He would never know.

So, instead of improving his mood, the walk round the property and the thoughts that accompanied it only left Eamonn in a worse mood than he had been in before.

'I'll be needing the Jeep keys.'

Colleen jumped when his voice sounded behind her. Glancing over her shoulder at his stern face, she nodded at Lorna, the more senior of the yard grooms. 'That's grand Lorna. He's a lot sounder on that foot today. Get the farrier to go ahead and put shoes back on him.'

As the girl disappeared up the yard with the gleaming horse, Colleen turned to face Eamonn. A quick glance over his face, steely-gazed and tight-lipped, told her what she needed to know. He was mad about something. It was in the set of his jaw, the tense line of his shoulders, the folded arms across his broad chest.

With a steadying breath she started to walk past him. 'There isn't a Jeep. We sold it.'

'Well, how do you get the heavy stuff, then?'

She glanced sideways as he fell into step beside her. 'We get it delivered. When there's call for it.'

Eamonn did a quick job of reading between the lines. 'Which isn't too often, is it? Because this place obviously can't afford the expenditure.'

'We have to prioritise. And the horses' welfare comes first.'

'Part of their welfare is decent grazing and safe boundary fences.'

She glanced again. 'Read a book on horses, did we?'

He ignored the jibe. 'You want this place to make money, Colleen, then it needs to look the part. And right now it looks like no one has given a damn in a long while.'

'*I* give a damn.' She stopped dead and spun on him, her eyes glittering dangerously. He had *no idea*. 'You have no idea what it means to care about this place like I do! What you're doing is trying to ease your guilt for not being here before your dad died by making it look pretty now. And it's *not* necessary.'

The accusation stung. Angry as he already was, it was the wrong thing for her to have said. He stepped in closer, his chin lowering, so that his clipped words washed over her face with his warm breath. 'If I were you I'd feel equally as guilty at this place being the way it is.'

Colleen paled visibly, her eyes widening in shock.

So close on the heels of his own self-deprecation, Eamonn fought jibe with jibe. 'All these years and you never *once* thought to tell me what he was hiding from me. That makes you every bit as irresponsible as he was for not asking for help.'

'Because you were so easily accessible, weren't you? Because it wouldn't have been going behind your dad's back, would it? Because everything is just so cut and dried to you! When you have no idea—no idea at all. Because you…*you* weren't here, dealing with all this! And *I was*!'

She couldn't help it. Tears welled in her eyes, her throat aching with the effort of holding them back. It was just too much. Even when Eamonn losing his temper with her was what she had been preparing for for weeks.

But after last night…

Turning her face from his, she focused on the yard cat, cleaning itself on the warm cobbles a few feet away. Focusing completely on it and nothing in her peripheral vision until she had enough control to speak.

When she did, her voice was still hoarse as it broke free from her raw throat. 'It wasn't in trouble for a long time. While your dad was alive he may not have been able to do the heavy stuff, but he still watched over everything. The place was still immaculate. All this is more recent.'

There was a brief moment of tense silence, then, 'How recent, exactly?'

'It started inside the year.' Her shimmering eyes risked

another brief glance in his direction while she floundered on the truth. She'd had no right to snap at him the way she had, and she knew it. But then it wasn't as if she'd rehearsed how she'd tell him the truth. If he hadn't come back she'd thought about writing a letter. But she'd hoped to find a solution to make things right by then. Some way of making amends.

The silence between them was deafening.

While she tried to form words, he did the last thing she'd expected him to do. His angry gaze softened, his mouth opened to take a deep breath, then he looked upwards, as if he was making a conscientious effort to stay calm.

When he looked at her again, he was back in control, with an even, if somewhat dull tone to his deep voice.

'It's not your fault. I *don't* blame you. You had a baby on the way, a sick man to look after. Something had to give. It's nothing that can't be fixed. But we have to be able to talk about this stuff calmly—both of us.'

Her breath caught in her chest at his words. He still had no idea. How could he possibly know what she had had to deal with? That most of it was indeed *her fault.* So reasoning with her wasn't going to help any, was it?

Somehow she managed to choke the words out. 'You don't understand.'

'What I understand is that it's unfair to march over here and give out to you the way I just did. I'm usually much better at negotiation than this. And maybe you're right. Part of it probably *is* guilt. I should have been here. I could have helped. You shouldn't have had all this responsibility on your own.'

'No, *Eamonn*…' She forced herself to step back a little from him, to tilt her chin so she could look up into his eyes.

But her words faltered as he stepped close again, raising his hands to her upper arms. His fingers spread wide for a second, then he wrapped them around so that his thumbs almost touched his forefingers, before squeezing gently to hold her attention. And the golden flecks in his eyes glowed fiercely as he tipped his head so close that Colleen couldn't think any further than how little effort it would take to touch her mouth to his.

If she had thought he was intense when she'd been fifteen, then this was way, *way* past intense.

Her heart stopped for a beat, then fluttered and beat rapidly to make up for the brief pause.

His dark lashes lowered slightly, shadowing his eyes as they moved over her face and hesitated at her parted lips. He then took another long breath, before he looked back up into her eyes and stared silently.

Colleen swallowed hard. Oh, this was not good. Not now. She couldn't go getting attracted to him again *now*.

'We can fix this. If you can try not to be so defensive around me, I can agree to try and do the same.'

She swallowed again. *What?* What had they been talking about?

His thumbs moved against her arms. 'We'll get the place tidied up and looking right again. Back to the way it used to be.'

Oh, yes. Now she remembered. She *had* to explain to him. There wouldn't be a better time. But even as she admitted that to herself, and summoned up the courage to speak, she also knew that by doing so she would be pushing him away. He would never again reach out the hand of friendship to her the way he just had—wouldn't look at her again with such intensity and warmth.

Never in her life would she be so close to fulfilling the dreams of her youth. Inches away from the first kiss that had haunted her for years. But the one that might have been possible for a fleeting second only moments before would have to remain a dream.

She had to tell him.

'I need to tell you something.' She twisted her arms and tried to move back again, to put some distance between their bodies. Because, in theory, it would hurt less if she was the one who did it.

But he held on, squeezed his hands tighter as he ordered, 'Shut up, Colleen.' He smiled. 'For once. *Enough*. You don't have to explain anything to me. What's done is done. Now we move forward. We do something pro-active about this place.'

And with that he let go, stepped back, and added, 'I'm going to put an order into the hardware store and get things started.' The smile was transformed to a grin. 'It'll do me good to have something to do.'

'But—'

'No buts. I'll enjoy it. It's been a while since I did this kind of thing.' His face seemed to get brighter with the thought of physical labour. 'Make me a list of what's needed on the yard for the horses too, and we'll get it ordered. Anything at all. I'll come back for it in an hour or so.'

Then, with a wink at her stunned expression, he turned and walked across the yard.

He was still smiling as he searched for a pen and paper to make his list for the hardware store. And he only stopped for a brief second to ask himself why.

The only answer that came to mind was that he hadn't been lying when he'd told her she wasn't on her own. She wasn't. He *was* there for her.

Until Colleen had her baby and was settled he wasn't going anywhere.

Something good had to come out of his past wrongs. He could fix something after all. It made him feel more like the good guy he wanted to be.

And doing something pro-active was a good thing too. Sitting around twiddling his thumbs wasn't something he was used to. He could spare a few weeks from his life to do something constructive. Well, something constructive was his thing, after all.

Maybe he could even make a friend out of it along the way, and leave Ireland knowing the closest person he had left to family was doing okay and could call him if she needed to.

His father would surely have approved of that.

CHAPTER SEVEN

THE man was a walking whirlwind. In the space of one afternoon he had lorry-loads of stuff ordered. Wood, nails, paint, fertiliser, weed spray, new wooden gates. And, for all Colleen knew, a partridge in a pear tree.

There was a steady stream of deliveries for the rest of the day. With more to come. And wherever there was unloading to do he was right in the thick of it, jumping onto the back of flatbed lorries and lugging around heavy bags as if they weighed nothing. All he needed was a cape and underpants outside his jeans.

And yet he looked happy as a pig in muck.

Which was surprising, when he didn't look like a pig. In fact he was way too nicely dressed to be doing what he was doing. Like some kind of ad for a male clothing company set in a farming scene for marketing purposes. His top-notch sweater and expensive jeans would never be the same again, would they?

Thing was, from her vantage point, a safe distance away, all the combination of his exuberance and good intentions did was make Colleen feel more and more guilty. Until it ate away at the pit of her stomach like a cancerous growth.

Walking into the office, when she couldn't watch him any longer or her heart would break, she commenced pacing up and down the old wooden floor. She had to tell him. No more stalling. No more reaching out for a warmth and consideration she didn't deserve.

She owed him the truth. He was trying so hard to do something good, to help her, even reach out the hand of friendship. Because she knew it wasn't out of a deep and abiding sense of love for Inisfree. And it couldn't be to try and make amends to the father who was gone. No, he was trying to look out for *her*, surreal as that was.

And she couldn't let him do it.

Rubbing her hand over her stomach, she tilted her head and rehearsed out loud. 'Eamonn, I need to tell you the truth about this place…'

She stopped and frowned. 'No. That's no good… Eamonn, it's not that I don't *appreciate* what you're doing…'

One hand flung out to her side. *For crying out loud!* Appreciate what he was doing? All he was doing was protecting his half of Inisfree. She couldn't stop him from doing that. After all, it was his legacy as well as hers. They were partners now—just as their fathers had been when they'd bought the run-down farm and turned it into one of the most reputable small studs in the country. He was doing exactly what *she* would have done if it had been within her capabilities. But even if she thought that was all he was doing, that it was nothing to do with taking care of her, she still couldn't stand by and let him fix it without knowing how it had got that way.

It had never occurred to her that he would want to come back and help run the place. She had always assumed, as Declan had, that he would be a silent partner. That at worst he would offer his half to Colleen at a low rate. It had been what she'd hoped would happen. *Before*.

Before Adrian had siphoned off all the money and headed into the sunset with a girl barely hitting twenty.

She paced again. 'It's like this, Eamonn. That idiot I was engaged to took all the money, and I was dumb enough to bring him here and trust him in the first place. It's all my fault, you see. Even though he was a useless son-of-a—'

The baby moved suddenly and she stopped. Smoothing her hand over her stomach again, she crooned, 'Shhh, baby. It's all right. Your father being useless isn't your fault.'

There was a sudden tightening across her distended midriff. Uncomfortable. Unexpected. And she froze.

What in hell was *that*?

The discomfort built, and was accompanied by a dragging sensation in her pelvis.

'Oh, *no*. Not now.'

And of course Eamonn chose that moment to walk in on her. 'That's the last load stored away. I was just wonder—' He stopped dead a few steps from her and his eyes widened. 'What's wrong?'

Colleen stared at him with large eyes, her voice coming out all small and helpless—which she hated. 'I don't know.'

He swore viciously, and was in front of her in one long stride, his hands reaching out, hesitating, and then folding around her elbows. 'Are you in labour?'

'How in hell would *I* know?' She glared at him. Though in fairness she *should* have known. She'd assumed she *would* know what labour felt like. But this? This just didn't feel right.

After a quick scowl, Eamonn glanced around the office, as if salvation was to be found amongst the chaos. Then he seemed to come to a decision, and began to push her back towards the desk. 'Maybe you should lie down?'

Her backside bumped off the desk-edge and she grimaced. 'On the desk? You want me to give birth on an *office desk*?'

'No, don't be dumb.' He scowled again. 'Sit down, then— here.' He steered her around the desk, glancing frequently at her as if she might shatter before his eyes. With extreme care he lowered her into the chair, and only then released her elbows. 'There—that's better.'

A wave cramped her stomach and she pursed her lips.

Eamonn grimaced, raking his long fingers back through his hair as he stared at her stomach. 'Another one?'

'Same one, I think.' Her lashes flickered upwards as she looked at his face. 'I'm not due for another two weeks.'

'Well, they can come early sometimes, can't they?'

'You're an expert now?' Her eyebrows rose. 'There's obviously been more to your time away than I thought.'

Pursing his lips in a mirror of hers, he shook his head, then hunkered down to look her in the eye. 'We should call for Dr Donaldson.'

Colleen laughed a low laugh. 'You'll need to shout pretty loud. He died five years ago.'

'Well, hell, Colleen, how would I know that?'

Grimacing again, she leaned back in the seat and tried to rub at the taut wall of her stomach with her hand. She really did need to stop being so defensive around him. He couldn't do any more than he was doing—couldn't be any more thoughtful and considerate if he tried. She forced herself to breathe deeply, to calm her voice. 'You wouldn't. Of course you wouldn't. I was kidding.'

'I know you were.' He rocked back and forth on his heels a couple of times, then reached out and enfolded her spare

hand in both of his, his voice dropping as he aimed a devastatingly sensual smile at her and whispered gruffly, 'Let me
call whoever *is* the doctor, then—to be on the safe side. For
my wellbeing if not for yours.'

He was right. She couldn't take a chance with her baby.
So she nodded, and pointed him at the phone book on one
edge of the desk, then waited while he stood, flicked through
the pages and dialled the number. His voice on the phone was
steadier than the gaze he constantly flickered back to her.

Then he was hunched in front of her again, his gaze warm
as he reclaimed her hand. 'He'll be here in a half-hour. Tell
me what I can do 'til then.'

Oh, damn it to all hell. She really couldn't take it when he
was warm and caring. Not when it was being aimed at her with
a smile that sent a tingle up her spine the way this one did.

Smiling a tremulous smile of her own, she rubbed again
at her stomach. 'You could sit with me a while? Take my
mind off it 'til the doctor gets here with tales of going to
America?'

'But what if you're *really* in labour?'

'Then we'll know soon enough.'

Hazel eyes dropped to her smoothing hand, and he stared
for a long, long moment. Just when Colleen thought he might
argue, and force her to actually lie on the desk, he started to
talk, his voice an even, deep grumble that distracted her from
her discomfort.

'I'd never seen so many tall buildings. It makes you feel
small, and very alone, when you first get there. I wanted to
come home about a dozen times the first couple of months,
after the novelty wore off and I'd seen all the sights. But—'

'But you were too stubborn to quit?'

When he looked up into her eyes he smiled. A soft,

genuine smile that warmed the gold in his eyes. 'Yeah, I was. I'd made such a fuss about going that to have come back with my tail between my legs less than three months later would have killed me.'

Colleen continued to smile in reply.

Eamonn laughed a low laugh. 'I guess you know that about me too?'

She gave a sage-like nod.

To which he shook his head, his gaze dropping again, this time to where he held her hand in his. He opened his fingers a couple of inches and let his thumbs graze back and forth over her knuckle. His smile hidden from her gaze, he shrugged his shoulders and continued. 'I worked on building sites the first year—learned everything I could about everyone else's job as well as my own. Bugged the hell out of foremen to learn what they did. And then I met Pete, and he took me under his wing.'

'Who's Pete?'

He glanced up briefly to answer. 'My partner. We set up the company together.'

Colleen studied the curls on his head for a long moment when he looked back down at their hands. She focused on finding two curls that curled in the same direction, on counting the different shades from chocolate to russet-brown. 'What's he like?'

'Gulliver in Lilliput.' He grinned as he glanced up again. 'He's six feet five.'

'No, he's not!' She laughed a low laugh. 'No one's that tall.'

A nod. 'Yep. Only guy who could ever hold me back in a bar brawl after a few too many jars. He thinks I fight like a five-stone weakling.'

'And I'll bet you tried swinging for him the first time he said that?'

'Hell, yes.'

'How'd you do?'

'He floored me like a five-stone weakling.'

She laughed again. 'I'd have liked to see that.'

'Well, I for one am glad you didn't.' He looked back at her hand. 'I'd prefer it if you just kept on seeing me as all-male.'

Not a problem there.

She was blinking innocently when he glanced up yet again, his eyes twinkling. 'Now, if you'd been there when I took on the McNally twins…'

'It's as well you had Pete to keep you out of prison.'

'We had some good times, all right.'

'I'll bet.'

He continued to smile up at her, his thumbs grazing back and forth, back and forth. So that the only thing Colleen could focus on was the rhythmical touch. How the warmth that touch created was gradually working its way up her arm to tingle over her sensitive breasts. And the way that his eyes shone up at her. It just wasn't fair.

She stared back at him, tears welling in the corners of her eyes. No amount of effort at blinking them away seemed to be working. So she tried to smile through them.

But Eamonn's steady gaze was observant. His thumbs stilled, his smile fading as he asked in a low rumble, 'What's wrong? Is it bad again?'

Her head shook in denial.

'Then what is it?'

In the face of such genuine concern she crumpled. How could he know it had been for ever since anyone had shown her such open concern? Had felt the need to offer warmth and comfort? It was her own fault, she supposed. Nine times out of ten she was so busy getting on with everything, making do with what life had dealt her, hiding her moments of weakness or depression behind closed doors. People probably just assumed she was doing grand. That she didn't need comfort or support. As if she was invincible or something.

But she was only human.

And this was Eamonn. The one person in the world she shouldn't have sought comfort from. Let alone felt such a sensual awareness of.

His hands closed around hers again and he squeezed. 'Hey, c'mon, now. None of that. You're fine. I'm here. And the doctor will be here soon, won't he? You'll be fine. I'll look after you, I promise.'

A small sob broke free, and she whimpered at the sound of it, pursing her lips together as she shook her head. Then she managed a small squeak. 'No, you don't understand.'

'Try me.'

It wasn't easy. But somehow she managed to tug her hand free and push her body up out of the chair. It wasn't graceful, and if Eamonn hadn't stood up and got out of her way she might not have had enough space to manage it.

But then she was on her feet, silent tears escaping her eyes, her chest cramping painfully, and she still couldn't find the words. She sobbed, got angry with herself for crying in front of him, then looked up into his worried face and sobbed again. She waved a hand aimlessly in the air and managed a choked, 'I have to go. I need— I just need a *little*...' she made a space between her thumb and forefinger in front of her body '...minute.'

'Okay.' He blinked at her with a frown, obviously discomforted by the sight of a hysterically crying female. 'Do you want me to—?'

'No-o.' She waved her hand again. 'I just need—I mean—I can't—' She swallowed, her voice lowering to a squeak. 'I just need a wee minute.'

Still blinking, Eamonn watched as she fled the room. What was going on?

After a few minutes of stunned silence he shook his head. And followed her.

CHAPTER EIGHT

SHE didn't reappear for hours after the doctor had visited. And although she had been silent during his examination, and the doctor had declared that everything was fine before he left, Colleen sobbed for a good while afterwards.

Eamonn hated hearing women cry—even when they tried to do it in private, and quietly. And one of the things he hated the most about it was how helpless he felt. What he tended to do was go and hand them a handkerchief. He was one of the very few men left on the planet who still carried one of the cotton varieties—a throwback to his dad, he suspected. Handing over a handkerchief and maybe patting a hand on a shoulder was as far as it went for him.

He'd never actually felt any pain himself because of it. But the capable, feisty Colleen breaking down like that…

Well, it had deeply affected him. Had opened a hole inside him that soon felt like a gaping wound. And he just wanted to fix the problem, whatever it was. He wanted to find a way to make things better for her. He just wasn't sure how.

Being a man of action, he decided to do some research while he waited for her to reappear. So he made coffee, turned on his laptop, and Googled *pregnancy*.

In the background he could still hear far-off muffled sobbing. Telling himself he would give her twenty minutes to get it out of her system or he was going up there to talk it out, he started reading.

After a while the sobbing became subdued, the house went silent, and only the hum of his laptop filled the air as he read on, his coffee going cold.

Dear Lord in heaven. Why did women *have* babies? Had they any *idea*?

When he'd got a crick in his neck looking sideways at pictures he'd accidentally opened of women giving birth, he'd had enough. Rising from his chair, he threw his coffee into the sink and then went to the bottom of the stairs to listen for sounds.

Nothing.

So he wandered into the family room and turned the TV on. But after flicking back and forth through the eight-odd channels available to him, he couldn't find anything to distract him enough.

Another quick listen at the bottom of the stairs. Still silence. She must have sobbed herself to sleep. *Damn it.*

He was almost on the first step, heading upwards to peek in on her, when his eyes fell on the other door across the hall. His dad's study. The last place he'd seen the old man before he left. Where he had seen the disappointment on his face after the exchange of harsh words before leaving the room to pack a bag. To call a taxi. To catch a plane. And to leave the land of his birth.

He'd never forgotten that last look on his dad's face. Had never given either of them the chance to apologise face to face.

With a breath he stepped forward, hesitating in front of the wooden door. It was almost as if he still felt he should knock—that he was still the teenager who had taken weeks to find the guts to tell his dad he wanted to leave. Then he took a breath and pushed open the door.

Colleen slept until the baby moving woke her up again. Disorientated at first, she soon remembered what a scene she'd made in front of Eamonn, and moaned aloud. Never, at *any* stage of her life, had she been a weeping female.

Not without due cause.

Bottling up all the emotion after Adrian's deception and the harsh words he'd spoken before he left, after having to tell Declan what he'd done and facing the ultimate repercussions of having broken his already weak heart, she had managed on her own while she grew large with her baby.

Bottling up all that had been bound to lead to a breakdown at some point. If only it hadn't been in front of Eamonn…

Eamonn who she had to be strong in front of when she told him the truth. So she could take all he'd have to say.

It was time. It was long since time.

She took a few moments to wash her face, to brush her hair into place, to smooth her crumpled clothes. And then she went to find him.

'Ah, so you're awake. Feeling any better?'

She stared at the sight of him in Declan's chair, the son so like his father in many ways. And her heart caught. It was so unfair that they'd never had a chance to really know each other, to get to spend time together while Declan was still around. Eamonn had missed out on so much.

And maybe if he had been there earlier, when all the trouble had begun, he could have done something to stop her from taking the path to destruction. His father had been too tired most of the time for her to burden him with her growing doubts. And by the time she had known it had been too late. But if Eamonn had been there…*maybe*…

More maybes.

She finally found her voice again. 'Yes, thank you. Much better.' Her cheeks warmed. 'I'm sorry about earlier. It's not like me to be so emotional. I was just—'

Eamonn raised a large hand to halt her. 'Oh, you don't have to explain—really. I did some research online, and it's a miracle you're not crying every five minutes. Not when you know what you've got coming, bringing that little kid into the world. I'd be a basket-case.'

He'd done *research*?

'You did *research*?'

His eyes shone with amusement from across the room, 'It's what men do. The practical option is always our escape route. We look at things from a practical view-point. Mull over all the information in our minds so we have answers at hand. Whereas, in general, women are ruled by their hearts.'

One fair eyebrow rose at his words. 'Oh, is that so?'

It wasn't that she necessarily disagreed with him. It was just the fact he'd said it the way he had, with that look of amusement in his eyes. She suddenly felt as if she was a lesser being for the very fact she had followed a heart which had led her down the wrong path. Instead of thinking a bit more.

A smile flashed briefly across his lips before he went back to flicking over some thick pages, his brow furrowing in concentration. 'I found some stuff of Dad's.'

He had? Colleen's breath caught until she realised he wasn't looking at an account book. Braving a few steps closer, she looked down at what it was that had him so fascinated. 'His photo album. He loved that album—looked at it practically every day.'

Eamonn looked up in surprise, having already been caught by the fact that the album contained more than just pictures of gleaming horses. Which was what he had been expecting when he'd found it. Instead he had found a photographic history of his parents' relationship and of his own childhood. Looking at it had brought him a range of emotions. Happiness at the earlier shots; poignancy at scenes he remembered from his childhood; sadness at the relationship that hadn't worked; regret that he'd forgotten so much.

To think his father might have felt the same things while looking at it made him feel closer to the man, yet tore him up at the same time. 'Every day since when?'

Colleen shrugged in answer, as if the question wasn't that big a deal. 'Since as long as I can remember. It was always on the desk, or by the box of your stuff that he kept.'

At the latter, Eamonn's features froze. Thick dark lashes blinked a couple of times as a scowl created a deeper furrow on his forehead—so deep a furrow that it suggested he frowned often. '*What* box of my stuff?'

Colleen was surprised by the second question, surprised by the note of disbelief in his voice. 'He kept a box of all the things you sent him, and any news he heard. He started it not long after you left. It's here somewhere…'

'Where?' He pushed back from the desk as she looked around, his head turning from side to side as he searched the room. 'What does it look like?'

'About that big.' She held her hands out to a fish-that-got-away size. 'And made of cardboard. It won't be far away—*ah*. There it is.'

Eamonn's gaze followed her pointing finger to the bottom

of a bookcase. Immediately he stepped over to lift the box and place it on the desk-top. Then, as Colleen walked closer to glance over his shoulder, he lifted the lid.

His large hand froze for a few seconds, and then he reached out and lifted a small shield.

Colleen smiled behind him. 'Fastest Runner.'

Eamonn nodded, his head bowed. 'Last year at primary school.'

He set it to one side and reached again, this time unfolding a square of newspaper. 'I'd forgotten this.'

She hadn't. 'School dance with Sheelagh McCartney. Weren't you the handsome one, in your bow tie?'

If he smiled she couldn't see it. But his hand faltered as he pushed photos and certificates to the side and produced a magazine. He hesitated, then flicked through until he found the article. It was a write-up and a photograph of the young entrepreneur who had taken New York's construction industry by storm, finding areas to develop before they became popular, making a fortune along the way.

A younger Eamonn smiled up at him from the glossy pages. He could remember clearly the day the photo had been taken, the sense of achievement he'd felt.

When he remained silent, Colleen spoke, her voice soft and steady. 'He was so proud of you. Never stopped telling everyone what a success you'd made of yourself. You achieved more in a few years than he felt he had in a lifetime, and it made the decision to let you go a little easier for him. Even though he missed having you around.'

She could have no idea of the effect her words had. Eamonn was frowning hard at the magazine, his fingers tightening on the edges as he fought to keep control. When he spoke his words were tight, forced out. Because he'd held them inside for so long.

'He could have said so to me. That might have helped.'

'But he did.' She was frowning in confusion when she moved round to look up into his face. 'I heard him on the phone with you when he told you how happy he was you were doing well for yourself.'

Eamonn's smile was forced, didn't make it all the way up into his eyes. 'I thought he was just saying it because he felt he had to. Maybe to cover up how disappointed he was at my not staying here. I let him down by leaving. I know that. It was his dream to have me here, like you were for your dad.'

Colleen swore softly, and he glanced at her with a look of surprise. She shook her head, stunned by his interpretation, and without thinking reached out for his arm and squeezed it in reassurance.

'No. You can't think that. He would never have had you do something you didn't love just out of duty to him. Surely you know that? It was just you being so far away that hurt him the most. Well, that's what I think. He never really re-covered from the fight you had the day you left. He felt guilty that that was the last memory you both had of each other.'

She smiled, looked down at her hand on his arm, and released it as suddenly as she had reached for him.

When she looked up, Eamonn nodded slowly with an understanding born of shared experience. He'd had the same regrets himself, after all.

Then he looked back down at the box, setting the magazine to one side as he discovered another newspaper, with a piece on a historic building being converted into apartments. Not reading the words, in the silence of the

comfortable room, he confided in someone for the first
time in a long time. 'We both said a lot of things we regretted that day. I know I did. We had the same quick
temper, as well as the same stubborn streak. It took that
first heart attack for me to pick up the phone. He never
would have.'

'He would have.' Her voice was still soft. 'You just beat
him to it, that's all.'

His chin rose again, his face turning to hers, his eyes locking
with hers. And the smile that he gave her spoke of a simple,
genuinely felt gratitude for her words. She almost melted. It
was as if somehow she had said something that he had really
needed to hear aloud. And she smiled in understanding. In
knowing the father, she was recognising something in the son.

And she was glad she could tell him what he obviously
needed to hear.

A flicker of something crossed Eamonn's eyes, and he
glanced at the newspaper in his hand, then back at
Colleen's face. His eyes narrowed in suspicion. 'How did
he *get* this stuff?'

Colour immediately flamed on her face.

Comprehension widened his eyes. '*You* sent for all this
for him? *How?*'

Her mouth opened, then closed. She glanced down,
avoiding his intuitive eyes. 'I…er…*well…*' Then she
scowled, her tone defensive. 'You're not the only one who
can use a computer, y'know.'

There was a brief pause while he ignored the edge to her
voice. 'You followed my career? Researched me? Sent for
magazines and newspapers?'

'Yes.' Her chin rose defiantly as she challenged him to find
a problem in that. But she avoided his eyes, chose a point

over his left shoulder to focus on. 'I thought your dad should see how you were doing.'

'You did, did you?'

'Yes.' Her body language gave her away, and she shook her head slightly while she said yes, making a lie out of the word. So she looked him straight in the eye and silently challenged him to call her on it. 'He really got into it. Even learnt how to use a search engine about a year ago. It was a weekly task for him.'

'But you originally started looking on *his* behalf, did you?' The gold glowed knowingly in his eyes.

'Yes!' The word came out louder than necessary.

His smile was slow. Devastatingly sensual. It told her that he knew better, that she'd been caught in her lie.

She laughed sarcastically in return, waggling her finger in warning. 'Ah, no, you don't, Eamonn Murphy. I had better things to do with my time than moon around after you when you left.'

'Meaning you mooned after me when I was *here*?'

Colleen froze, her mouth slightly open. She'd just dug a deep hole, hadn't she?

Eamonn set the paper down and turned to fully face her, his belt buckle hitting against her distended stomach. 'Did you, Colleen? Did you moon after me? Is that why you started looking me up to see how I was doing?'

Any minute now she would find a suitable sarcastic answer for that. Something to wipe the knowing look off his face. She would. But somehow, having kept the truth from him on so many other things, lying to him again was too much for her.

So she faltered.

She blinked several times as she thought of a way of

denying it. She dampened her lips with the tip of her tongue as his smile grew, her eyes widening when the action drew his gaze to her mouth.

Oh, heck.

His heated gaze remained on her parted lips as his voice came out on a low, seductive grumble. 'I had no idea. But then, there was a bigger difference between an eighteen-year-old and a fifteen-year-old than there is now.'

Even as she took a breath to ask what difference it would have made to the bigger picture, her heart caught.

He said, 'I guess I owe you an apology. And a thank-you for all the stuff you got. For *my dad*.'

He smiled knowingly. And then his head descended.

Oh, no.

Not now. Not ever, her heart cried, but especially *not now*!

She raised a hand to his chest, felt the hard heat of him as he pressed against it,

'Stop.' It nearly killed her to say it. Especially when she didn't want him to stop. Even if it only ever happened once in her lifetime…

He lifted his dark eyebrows in question.

She took a breath, her hand dropping away from the steady beat of his heart. 'I need to tell you something. And I really can't put it off any longer. I should have told you when you got here.'

CHAPTER NINE

EAMONN'S face told her many things in that instant. The raise of his brows told her he was curious, the spark in his eyes told her that he didn't want to stop, that he had indeed intended to kiss her, even if the impulse had only been there for a split second and it had been meant merely as a thank-you.

And the slight parting of his lips told her he was about to question her.

So she stepped back from him, put distance between their bodies, in a pre-emptive strike of sorts. Because, she tried to tell herself, it was better she move away from him rather than have the humiliation of him moving away from her. *Which he would.*

'I need to tell you about Adrian.'

Eamonn's mouth closed. He stared at her, then opened his mouth and asked, 'Who is Adrian?'

Colleen took a deep, bracing breath. 'My fiancé.'

It was like being gut-punched. Eamonn's eyes widened. 'You're engaged? You said you weren't.'

And if she was, then why lie about it? And, more to the point, where was he when she so obviously needed him?

She ran her tongue over her lips again, and he felt a scowl

appear on his face when he noticed it. Why was he so aware of everything she did? Of where she was looking, of the flicker of her long lashes, of the way she would tuck her hair behind her ear when she was unsettled? Or of how she was taking a breath before every sentence, the way she was right that second? A breath that would raise her lush breasts for just an instant and then lower them as she exhaled the words. Momentarily distracting his gaze from her face.

Why did he notice every little thing about her?

'I'm not. Not any more. I told you, he left.'

Eamonn surprised himself by exhaling, not having realised he was holding his breath. 'He's your baby's father?' The words left a bitter taste in his mouth. 'The one who took off with the stable girl? That one?'

A different kind of flush appeared on her cheeks as she avoided his gaze. 'Yes, that one.'

She began to pace in front of him, her hand smoothing over her stomach. So Eamonn turned around and leaned back against the desk, shoving his hands deep into his pockets. 'It's not really any of my business. And it really doesn't have anything to do with me wanting to kiss you.'

She froze, her back to him. Then she lifted her head and turned round again.

Eamonn took advantage of the brief pause to ask another question, forcing nonchalance into his tone and shrugging his shoulders to back it up. 'Unless you're still in love with him, and you thought a wee kiss with an old friend might be betraying him?'

The words brought a swift burst of sharp, nervous laughter. 'Oh, no, that ship has well and truly sailed.'

Another shrug. 'Then I don't see why I need to know about him.'

But even as he said the words he knew he was lying. He *did* want to know. He wanted to know what sort of a sleaze had got her pregnant, left her when she needed him most, left his own child and taken up with some adolescent female. Some lesser female who couldn't possibly be as fascinating as the normally feisty Colleen. Who would never have cared enough about a man who wasn't even her own father to have tried to mend bridges between him and his equally stubborn son. Like Colleen had.

The fact that she might have cared enough about the son to look out for his welfare too warmed Eamonn's heart. He *liked* that she'd cared enough to see what he was doing, to follow his career from a distance like some kind of guardian angel.

'You need to hear it. I wish you didn't. Really I do.'

The colour had drained from her cheeks, and Eamonn frowned even harder. He may want to know, but he didn't want her to tell him if it hurt her in the telling.

'Colleen—'

'*Please!*' Her voice was sharp as she held a hand in front of her body, palm towards him. 'Please don't interrupt me. Not now that I've finally got up the courage to tell you everything. I've wanted to. I really have. I just didn't know where to begin. It's—well, it's not easy for me. But you need to know.'

She was obviously determined to tell him one way or another. And even though the tremulous tone to her voice sent a shiver up his spine, he somehow knew he had to hear it. It was important to her. And that made it important to him. She had no idea of the gift she'd given him by telling him his father had been proud. He told himself listening was the least he could do in return.

'Go on.'

'He came highly recommended—'

'As a fiancé?'

Colleen scowled at what she perceived as his attempt at humour, even though he'd delivered it with a completely deadpan expression and a flat tone. 'As a yard manager. He'd worked on two racing yards in the West, and had a terrific CV. When he appeared we needed someone who could take care of the business end of things—help us to expand, build a website for the foreign breeders. That kind of thing.'

As Eamonn nodded briefly in understanding, his eyes narrowing, Colleen began to pace again, justifying what she was telling him. 'And he was just so charming when he arrived. *Everyone* liked him. And he seemed so open, like he could be trusted…'

'Is that why you fell for him? Because he was charming and trustworthy?' *Was that all it had taken?* Somehow Eamonn thought he'd think less of her if that was all it had taken. She owed more to herself. She deserved the whole package. Why would she settle for less?

Her face turned in his direction and she scowled in momentary confusion. 'What has that got to do with anything?'

Yet another shrug. 'Hardly hearts and violins, is it?'

She looked even more confused. 'What does it matter to you why I fell for him? It's got nothing to do with what I'm trying to tell you.'

'I'm just trying to get the bigger picture.'

The scowl became a deep frown, her expressive eyes hiding behind more confused blinking. Then she seemed to reach a decision, and sighed. But the reach of her hand to the stray strand of hair gave away her unease at the topic. Her eyes avoided his face again, looked around the room, and she tilted her head from side to side as she floundered.

And Eamonn read every little signal. Felt his unease rise as she continued.

'I don't know what it was. Not now that I know what kind of person he really is. But at the time he was—I don't know—just *fun* to be around. He was so enthusiastic about this place, he cared about it the same way I did, and it just— *made sense*. That's all. He fitted into my life.'

Was everything that Eamonn wasn't. He could read that between the lines without her saying it. It made him feel like a lesser man. Unworthy, almost. As if he had no right to have wanted to kiss her a few minutes ago, even on impulse. Which, he discovered, was a feeling he didn't much care for. He had nothing to feel guilty about, after all.

So his words were clipped as a result. 'Go on.'

With a brief glimpse his way, she did—and dropped the bombshell. 'I didn't know he was taking money until after I found out about Catherine. The girl he ran away with.'

There was a heavy pause. Then, as if a dam had been broken, it all came out in a rush of wobbling words.

'Two cheques bounced, and the bank rang to tell me. That's when I found out we were in real trouble. It was all a scam, you see. The money for the website, the money for equipment, the advertising, the investment in a new warm-blood stallion to improve the bloodlines. He made out all the cheques, and we—*I*—trusted that he was doing what he said he was.'

When she paused for breath Eamonn jumped in. 'That's why this place is in trouble now?'

'Yes.'

'And you didn't go to the police?'

She flushed again. 'No.'

'Why in *hell* not, Colleen? Did you really think you were

that in love with this bastard that you had to let him *go*? Scot-free?'

When he pushed upright from the desk to spit out the words Colleen flinched. For a second she looked as if she might fold, a wave of despair crossing her face. But then she squared her shoulders and looked him straight in the eye with her large sad eyes. 'I co-signed the cheques.'

'You did *what*?' Eamonn gaped in disbelief. 'How did he get you to do *that*?'

She swallowed, her throat convulsing as if she might genuinely be sick. 'I...he...well, he had all the paperwork, order forms and bills. So I signed the cheques to match them. I just—I just didn't think—'

Eamonn swore viciously, releasing his hands from his pockets and bunching them into fists. Oh, the guy was a pro. A real piece of work. Had seducing her been part of gaining her trust? Or had the opportunity just been too good to miss? *Son-of-a—*

Her getting pregnant must have really messed up his great plan! If Eamonn ever caught up with him—

'When I told Declan—' Her voice broke.

And Eamonn wanted badly to hit something. To throw things. To rage at the world for what she had been put through. Instead he managed to stand his ground, his fists gripped by his sides and his jaw so tight his teeth hurt.

Colleen cleared her throat. 'He tried so hard to help get the work done. He really did. Came out on the yard every day for a week after Adrian left. But it was just too much for him.'

Her voice broke again. And Eamonn froze. He could see it so clearly it was like a film playing across the eyelids he had closed. Dear God. What a mess. *He should have been here.*

'He—he collapsed in the yard. And—and he was—he was dead before they got him to the hospital.'

He opened his eyes and looked at her. All colour had drained from her face. Even her eyes had gone blank. As if she wasn't even in the room with him any more, but had gone back in time to five months ago. When Declan Murphy had died. While his son had stood looking at temples in the sunshine of Peru.

Eamonn couldn't listen to any more. He stared at the tears that were streaking down her pale cheeks. Any wonder she'd been so upset that day, had been so defensive with him when he'd mentioned the state of the yard! She'd held all this inside, had had to go through all this on her own.

She hadn't been the one who had embezzled the money and put Inisfree on the ropes. *She* hadn't forced his father to come out and try to do the small things that, even though they'd proved beyond him, in the end wouldn't have made a bit of difference to the bigger picture.

And yet here she was, shouldering the responsibility of telling Eamonn what had happened. How she had been used, humiliated and abandoned. It should never have happened to her. Colleen didn't deserve all this.

When she took a breath to steady herself, to find the strength to speak again, he stopped her. 'That's enough. It's more than enough.'

She dropped her chin and nodded. So that she didn't see the look on his face as he stared at her.

'I need some time to calm down, Colleen. I'm sorry,' And he really was. Sorry that he wasn't a strong enough man to put his anger at a complete stranger to one side long enough to offer her comfort.

Sorry would have to do in the meantime; 'til he calmed down, got control.

He'd never in his life been so angry. But it wasn't Colleen he was angry at. It was himself.

CHAPTER TEN

COLLEEN had prepared herself for anger, for shouting and re-crimination and disappointment. She'd told herself that was what she deserved from him. So, as much as she was capable, she had prepared herself for that. And more.

When he had confessed aloud that he *had* been going to kiss her she had almost folded there and then. Given in to the need to be kissed and held, if only for just a moment.

But it wasn't what she deserved. Not from Eamonn.

For a moment when his temper had risen, when he had asked her how it had happened, why she hadn't phoned the police, she had thought it was the beginning of the anger she had prepared for.

What she hadn't been prepared for was his deathly calmness as he walked past her. Or the echoing sound through the empty house when he slammed the back door.

And she most definitely hadn't been prepared for the sense of loneliness she felt when he was gone.

He'd been back—what?—three days? Or was it four? She couldn't remember. But while he'd been back, even while she'd been avoiding the inevitable, she hadn't been alone.

Now she was. Alone and empty. Drained of any emotion she had left, with only her thoughts to keep her company.

What now?

Inisfree was the only home she had—had ever known. Being around the horses was the only time her soul felt at peace. Would he even want her here now? Did she even have the right to be there? After she had brought poison into its midst? Stood blindly as it had taken hold and collapsed her world around her ears?

With those thoughts crashing around in her head she should have been a basket-case. But her emotional well was dry. She really had nothing left.

So she roamed through the empty rooms and eventually sat at the long table in the kitchen, a cup of sweet tea in front of her. And stared into space while it went cold.

It was almost dawn when he came back.

Dominating the doorway, he stared at her with slow blinks of his thick lashes. And said nothing.

There was just an awful silence. One that Colleen normally wouldn't have left alone. But it was his move now, all his. There wasn't anything more she could say or do.

Eventually he glanced away from her face, and closed the door behind him before walking to the sink. His back to her, he ran the tap and washed and washed at his hands.

Colleen waited, her back straight, aching from sitting in the one place for so long.

He turned off the tap, glanced briefly over his shoulder as he reached for a clean towel. And just when she thought she was going to get the silent treatment as the first stage of her punishment his voice sounded in a low grumble.

'Have you been up all night?'

She nodded, realised it was pointless because his back was to her, and managed an even-toned, 'Yes.'

He mirrored the movement silently, as if he'd already known the answer. Then he took a breath that lifted his wide shoulders before he turned around. 'We need to talk about this some more.'

She nodded again, her gaze dropping from his face to the mug of cold tea. 'Yes.'

With a moment's pause, he pulled the sleeves of his thick navy sweater back down, leaning back against the edge of the deep Belfast sink as his eyes fixed on the top of her bowed head.

Colleen knew he was staring without looking up because she could feel it; could feel her scalp tingle where he was looking. 'I get it if you feel you don't want me here any more, if you want me to leave. That's completely understandable. What I did—'

'What *you* did?' His voice rose in astonishment. '*You* didn't do anything.'

The sharp outburst astonished her, and her eyes shot up to lock with his. He was frowning. But it wasn't the same kind of angry frown she had witnessed hours before. This one spoke of incredulity. And Colleen didn't understand that, not one little bit.

'But I explained it to you. I told you—'

'You told me you got suckered by a complete scumbag. That was hardly your fault. Any more than my dad's heart attack could have been your fault.'

Hadn't he been listening to a single word she'd said?

'But I brought Adrian here. It was my idea. I *trusted* him. If I hadn't—'

'If you hadn't been the kind of warm-hearted person who

still trusted in people you might have been able to see what he was really like?'

Colleen gaped, her eyes wide.

Eamonn paused, his voice dropping an octave. 'It wasn't your fault.'

Her back screaming at her, she hauled herself up from the chair she had been in almost since he left, scowling at him across the room. 'You didn't listen to a word I said.'

'I've been listening to every word you've said since I came back here.' He frowned right back at her.

Colleen had done her crying, so the only place left to go was anger. How could he say that? How could he stand there so deathly calm and not hate her guts? If this was some form of cruel revenge then he could just forget it! Anger was preferable to understanding. Or to sympathy.

'No, you *haven't* listened. I can't believe you're this stupid. I *let* him do this! I stood by and believed everything he said to me without a second thought. If I'd spent more than five minutes looking at the bigger picture from the outside I would *never* have let this happen. And now because of me your father is dead!'

Eamonn didn't move for a long while as she shouted the words at him. But his face got darker, his jaw set in a firm line. His eyes were sparking at her, but devoid of any hint of anger or recrimination. Then he suddenly pushed away from the sink and marched towards her with a look of complete determination. Colleen visibly baulked.

She wobbled on her feet, stepped back. But she was too slow. He had hold of her upper arms in a firm grasp before she had time to move.

Closing the final couple of inches between their bodies, he surrounded her with his presence, dominating her with his size and his heat as he leaned his face in closer to clip out his words.

'Now, you listen to me, Colleen McKenna, and you listen good. If you have a fault in this then it's that you let your heart blind you to *his* faults, because you need to believe in the good in people. But I'm willing to lay money on the fact that he was damn good at what he did. He *played you*, right up to the end.'

'But your dad—'

'My dad had a bad heart. It could have quit any time.' He gripped her arms harder to emphasise his words. 'The work he did in that week wouldn't have made any difference to what happened. If we were really that alike, then I can under-stand why he would have tried. You wouldn't have been able to stop him, no matter what you did. It was what he wanted. And he died doing what he loved doing.'

After a brief examination of her eyes, his gaze flickering from one to the other, his grip softened, his voice softly persua-sive. 'I don't think a person can ask for much more than that.'

Colleen stared up at him, her heart catching in her aching chest. Why was he being so forgiving? She didn't get it. For months she had tortured herself over everything that had happened, had had sleepless nights as her mind played it over and over. She'd had to bury herself in work to try and rectify what she had let happen, tiring herself out so that she slept dreamlessly.

She had been so wrapped up in her own sense of guilt, and in the loss of someone who had meant so much to her since her own parents had died, that she had never looked at it from any other angle. In doing so she would have been making herself a victim. And she so didn't want to admit that she had been. That she had been so easily fooled.

Just when she'd honestly believed she wouldn't cry ever again, she felt herself having to fight back more tears. But she couldn't cry in front of him. Couldn't take a chance that he would once again try to offer her comfort.

Her strength was the only thing she had left. And he could take it from her so easily, with a look or a simple touch or with softly spoken sincerity.

But he wasn't done. 'You've spent months worrying about this, haven't you? With no one here to talk to about it while you went out on that yard and tried to keep this place going.'

She swallowed hard. She would *not* cry.

His grip had loosened, transformed into a soothing caress, his thumbs moving back and forth in a pattern newly familiar to her. And she clenched her teeth as he spoke, willing the tears to stay at the base of her throat and in the backs of her eyes.

'If I hadn't got here you'd have kept going until the minute you had this baby, and you'd have been back out there straight after, wouldn't you? Working yourself into the ground when you should have been concentrating on your child.'

Colleen knew she had to get away from him. She couldn't keep holding back. It just hurt too much.

But when she swayed away he held on. 'Well, no more. I mean it. You won't give that man any more than he's already taken by blaming yourself. I won't let you. So you can just stop blaming yourself. Starting now.'

Swallowing hard, she willed herself to speak in an even tone. 'You can't—'

'I *can*. Because you're the closest thing to family I have left. And I'll be damned if I'll stand by and watch you pay a penance for something that wasn't your fault.'

'*Eamonn*—' His name came out in a strangled whisper,

her breasts rising and falling close to his chest as she strove for enough air to give her the strength she needed to continue.

Rather than silence her with more words, he did the one thing she couldn't argue with. The one thing that would momentarily stun her into silence.

He leaned in and whispered her name back at her, his mouth hovering above hers. *'Colleen*. Shush.'

It wasn't a kiss of passion. No, nothing that straightforward. Passion she might have been able to fight against. And maybe he knew that. So instead it was a gentle touching of a firm mouth against soft lips that spoke of understanding and giving.

It was exactly the kiss she had imagined in all of her dreams, had wanted in her childhood fantasies. For their first time. A kiss that spoke of caring, of giving and understanding. A kiss meant to heal a thousand wounds.

She had just never imagined it would be so soul-shattering at the same time.

It was meant as a soothing kiss. One that, even though it lasted only a brief moment, was aimed towards easing long months of pain. It broke her in two. Because she would have wished for so much more from his kiss.

One hand let go of her forearm and he raised his head, his eyes glowing down at her.

'After all you did for my dad over the years, the very least I can do is help you out now. I owe you.'

He turned his hand over, raised his knuckles towards her face, but just before it smoothed along her cheek the sleeve dropped back, and her eyes caught the red marks.

They were so close to her face that she had to lean back to get a better look. Then her eyes shot to his, wide and full of accusation. 'What did you do to your hand?'

Eamonn's dark lashes flickered as he looked towards it, then lowered it to his side. 'It doesn't matter.'

'Yes, it does!' She leaned forward, grasped hold of his wrist, turned the hand over and pushed the sleeve back with her thumb, so she could study it more closely. And there they were, all along his knuckles and the backs of his long fingers. Angry, open grazes.

With a glance up at his face she scowled and reached for the other hand, glaring up at him. 'What did you do, you stupid man?'

He stared briefly down to where her small hands held his wrists, then up into her eyes with a wry smile. 'I may have worked off some of my anger in the feed shed before I went for a walk to think things through.'

Colleen swore and tugged on his wrists, steering him back to the sink. 'Of all the—'

'Don't say stupid again. You did well to even get away with it twice already.' When she released one wrist to turn the tap on, he tried to tug the other free.

But she tugged right back, her eyes determined as she glowered up at him. 'Well, getting your hands messed up like this *was* stupid. Really stupid.' She reached across him and opened a cupboard above his head, seeking out disinfectant and cotton wool. 'Out there, taking your temper out on my poor feed bags, when you should have—'

He swiftly turned the wrist she still held and captured hers, squeezing in warning. 'You'd better not even *think* I should have come in here and taken it out on you.'

The sudden turn of dominance in his favour caught her unawares, as did his insight into her thoughts. Her long lashes flickered up to his face, then away, as she focused her attention on holding his other hand under the running water.

His deep voice softened. 'Is that really what you thought I'd do?'

She continued focusing on her task, so he squeezed her wrist again, 'Have you that low an opinion of me?'

When he squeezed again, demanding an answer, she shook her head. 'I didn't think you'd hit me, no. I'd never think that of you.'

'I should damn well hope not!'

Colleen blinked as the water ran over his knuckles and streamed through her fingers. She would never have believed he'd take his temper out on her—not physically. Even the tingle of his soft kiss still lying on her mouth spoke of tenderness, not anger. 'I was prepared for you to be angry—'

'I'll never be *that* angry.'

Risking a glance up into his eyes, she attempted to show him that she believed him by not hiding her thoughts from him as her voice dropped. 'I *know*. But this—' She took a breath and looked away again. 'This wasn't what I expected from you.'

Eamonn studied the top of her head while she switched hands and repeated the rinsing. He smiled a soft smile, studying her progress as she leaned forwards, and her hair slipped from behind her ear. 'You expected me to rant at you. Shout and yell and blame you as much as you'd already blamed yourself. Right?'

With a tilt forward he caught sight of her biting at her bottom lip between her straight teeth before she answered him with a low, 'Yes.'

The smile faded from his mouth, but remained in his eyes as she risked an upward glance. 'Guess you can't tell all that much about someone's personality from newspaper clippings over the years, then, can you?'

His teasing words raised a brief smile. Which he answered

with an intense gaze that set her blood racing before she
found the strength to turn away.

Then he spoke. 'Truce?'

She exhaled, and nodded. 'Okay.'

After a long, electric moment Colleen concentrated fully
on the task of his hands, and Eamonn allowed her to—until
the first time she swabbed him with disinfectant. 'Whoa—
that hurts, y'know!'

A smile came through in her voice. 'Don't be such a
baby.'

'Oh, you're going to be one hell of a mum.' He swore
when she dabbed again. Snatching his hand back, he glared
down at her when she turned round. 'Lord help the poor kid
if he ever gets anything in his eye.'

She surprised them both by laughing. And Eamonn
grinned in response, reaching his stinging hands out to catch
hold of her shoulders, sensing he'd broken the tension.
'That's more like it. Now, if you make us a cup of tea, I might
even tell you what I came up with to get everything sorted
out. Because we can do this. You and me. *Together.*'

CHAPTER ELEVEN

SHE was fading by lunchtime. She could feel it. Only to be expected after such an emotional rollercoaster over the space of twenty-four hours, added to the fact that her sleep pattern was now officially messed up.

Over a pot of tea Eamonn had laid out his plan, attempting to be masterful along the way. Which Colleen appreciated. *She did.* But at the same time it had been a long, long time since anyone had felt the need to take care of her. And she wasn't sure she was entirely comfortable with it from *him*...

Especially after his brief kiss.

When he had started to speak again she had found it hard to meet his gaze, despite their moment of laughter. Because the little voice in the back of her head that she had ignored during the whole Adrian debacle had been shouting loud and clear. It was her warning bell. And she now knew better than to ignore it again. What it had been telling her was that she knew what she had felt as a teenager with a starry-eyed crush might have grown less starry-eyed, but it hadn't disappeared completely. And with each thoughtful thing Eamonn did, with each facet of his personality that was slowly being revealed to her, she was rapidly growing a more adult version of the crush. Which really wasn't that great a plan. Not at all.

'So.' He had leaned forward over the table with a determined look. 'After this, you're going to get something to eat and you're going to get some sleep. You need your rest now.'

'But it'll be morning stables soon—' she stubbornly protested, even while she knew he was right.

'I don't care. I'll help the girls and get everything done that needs to be done.' He smiled at her look of disbelief when she risked a glance at his face. 'I'm a big boy. I can manage.'

Colleen didn't doubt that for a minute. But she was astounded that he would even try. And on *her* behalf.

'You need to concentrate on looking after yourself.' He pointed a long finger at her stomach. 'And that baby in there. That's your priority right now. I can look after everything else.'

'But the finances—'

He interrupted her again, and Colleen started to get pretty annoyed with that. Only afterwards would she see it as his way of trying to lay down the law, to be in control. Which she would later admit was sweet. Kind of. In a very male way.

'Now, you're on *my* turf with that problem.' He smiled. '*That* I can fix.'

Words which brought her out of passive, understanding mode. 'I won't let you pour your money into this place. You worked hard for that money, and it's hardly like you're made of the stuff!'

His eyes sparkled at her in amusement. Which irritated the hell out of her. Was he babying her now? Was that his way of dealing with everything she had told him? Because if patronising her like a child who had made naïve mistakes rather than losing his temper with a woman who should have known better was his answer, Colleen honestly would have preferred his wrath.

'You shouldn't have to bail out this place after *I*—'

'I'm not. It can do it itself. The place has assets enough to get itself out of trouble...'

And just like that he had laid out his scheme for getting their shared legacy back on its feet.

Now, hours later, as she leaned back in the large chair in the office, fighting her heavy eyelids, Colleen was still stunned she hadn't thought of it herself.

At first she had assumed he meant to sell the horses. It wasn't as if he was fond of them. And she had told him point-blank, 'You *can't* sell the horses. Without horses there *is* no Inisfree. I can't let you do it.' It would have killed her to lose them.

Still smiling at her, he answered merely, 'Tempting as that may be, darlin', I have bigger plans. Your four-legged friends wouldn't make the same money as I have in mind.'

Colleen wanted to scream when he drawled the word 'darlin'' at her with such arrogance and then stopped talking, pinning her eyes with a steady, confident stare. She just couldn't understand him—couldn't read him or predict what he would do next. When she expected him to go left he went right, and it was exhausting.

But she wouldn't be patronised or made to feel like a child either.

'When I drove here the first day it struck me how many new houses there are being built. The place is really starting to take off, construction-wise.'

Colleen nodded, her brain still slow to kick into gear at that stage. 'Yeah—young couples, mostly. We're within commuting distance of Dublin now, with the new motorways, and they find it cheaper to buy a plot of—'

He laughed as she put the pieces in place, her eyes widening. 'That's the girl. *Now* we're on the same page.'

That was a first. 'But we can't lose that much land.'

'We wouldn't have to. Three-quarters of an acre to an acre is a small plot. And two of those where the land touches the main road, with planning permission, should raise enough to get us out of trouble.'

And there it was. Just like that. A way out.

Which was why, even now, after her brain had had hours to look at things from every angle, Colleen was still asking herself *why* hadn't *she* thought of that?

It was so simple it was almost genius. A couple of acres were nothing if it saved the whole of Inisfree from going under.

He had found a way to save their legacy. To make the place work. Within a few short hours of being given the details for the first time. While she had struggled for months to find the same kind of miracle.

It made her feel like a *complete* idiot.

Never in her life had she considered herself the kind of woman who relied on a man to get her through the rough times. Thanks to having worked with horses from an early age, she had learned to be organised, efficient, observant— generally an all-round capable kind of a gal.

Until Adrian had knocked her down a peg or two.

It had taken blind belief in the wrong man to show her she wasn't infallible. To bring her confidence shattering downwards. She'd tried to fight through it, to keep going, to get from one day to the next.

Now it was another man—this time one she'd had no faith in when it came to love of the place—demonstrating to her that she should have been able to do more. A man who had already had her independence tested on a daily basis since his arrival by being thoughtful and strong, and having her *like* those things about him.

And, unreasonably, although she really did appreciate what he was doing, a part of her hated him for showing her another weakness along the way. For feeling the need to take over and make good on her mistakes.

'I'll have to find out about planning. How to apply and everything.' That had been her attempt at taking back some control, at showing him she could do something pro-active now that she had been shown a solution.

But Eamonn had simply shaken his head, folding his long arms over the table-top in front of him and leaning on them. 'No, I'll do that. That's what I do. And I'm damned good at it. I told you—you're on my turf now. So you just concentrate on looking after yourself 'til the baby comes. We'll talk again when things are more settled.'

She should have been relieved that he was taking things as well as he was, even if he *had* gone out to hit something because he was so angry. And he hadn't used it against her—hadn't read it as a way to get her out of Inisfree so he could pull it apart at the seams. Which should have made her feel grateful even if it wouldn't completely remove the sense of guilt she had been cultivating for so long before his return.

The thing was, much as she hated to admit it, she wanted to be better than she was. To have made better decisions and had a successful, thriving business for Eamonn to see. Because she would have quite liked to impress him. Just a little.

In an ideal world she would have been svelte, gorgeous, successful and confident. So that he would have looked at her and been bowled over by her on a personal level too. But it wasn't to be.

Colleen sighed as she allowed her eyelids to close for a few moments. Just the one time in her life it would have been nice.

The fact was, while he'd been away making a success of his life, she'd been at home making a mess of hers.

And there was bound to be some glamorous, successful woman waiting for him back in New York, wasn't there? Someone who *was* svelte, gorgeous, successful and confident. Someone Colleen could never hope to compete with. If she thought she could even catch his attention enough to make him interested in a contest in the first place.

A deep breath and she opened her eyes again, leaning forward in the chair to continue the list she'd been making of things that needed to be done with the horses.

She really needed to just wise up and get on with it. There was no point in wasting time hoping he would see something in her that he hadn't seen before. Maybe she was even fooling herself into believing she had something there at all. It was soul-destroying.

Eamonn would help her do what had to be done. He would put in all that work to knock Inisfree back into shape, to protect his half of the legacy. Maybe even seeing it as a nest egg for the future. But then he'd be gone again. And this time there wouldn't be any reason for him to come back. She'd known that from the start.

Colleen *knew* that was the way it was. What he was doing was already way more than she could ever have expected from him.

'If it works then Inisfree will pay you back what you spent on all that stuff the other day. It's only fair,' she had told him, while she decided to do what had to be done to allow him to leave.

There had only been the briefest hesitation, then he had nodded as he pushed back from the table. 'Let's just see what happens these next few months.'

Months—as in plural? The idea had rocked her.

'What about your work in New York?'

He had glanced briefly at his thick wristwatch. 'That's what I have a partner for. It's too early to call him now, so I'll try later. But he'll be fine. Pete's been doing it longer than I have. And he's an even bigger boy than I am, so he'll cope.'

When she had opened her mouth he had interrupted her yet again. If it hadn't been for the solutions he'd already revealed in such a short space of time Colleen would have pulled him on it. Simply because it bugged the hell out of her.

But he'd been around the table as he spoke, pulling her chair back and using his large hands to pull her upright. 'Now, enough chit-chat. It's off to bed with you. How am I supposed to get anything done with you under my feet?'

Still holding her elbows, he had leaned his face close to hers, his warm breath washing over her cheeks in sensual waves as his voice dropped to an intimate level. 'This will all turn out fine. I promise. You just have to trust me.'

Colleen remembered how she had blinked up at him, her heart heavy in her chest. In that moment she had wanted to be kissed again, to feel his mouth on hers. To have the right to want it. If she hadn't been so large with another man's baby she might even have initiated it—stepped in and reached her hands up into his thick hair to draw his head down to hers. To lose herself in a more mature version of her adolescent fantasies.

But what she had done was nod, drag her eyes away from

his warm gaze, then step back out of his hold. And she had promised herself there and then that she would work her behind off to put things right so that he could leave.

She just needed to remember that he *would* leave, and not allow her heart to hope once again that he wouldn't.

CHAPTER TWELVE

'So what is this woman like, then?'

Eamonn sighed at the question, his eyes focused on Colleen grooming a horse in the yard while he held the phone to his ear. 'Well, for starters she's probably the most stubborn female I've ever met. No matter how many damn times I tell her to rest, she just keeps on going.'

'How far along did you say she was?'

'When I got here she was a couple of weeks off her due date. So it must be close. Maybe even a little over by now.'

Pete's voice hinted at a smile. 'Marcy went way over with Shay—you remember that. Every time my cellphone rang I had a mini-heart-attack.'

And at the time Eamonn had ribbed him mercilessly about it. Suddenly it wasn't so funny any more. It was making him crazy, as it happened. Because it wasn't as if it was his kid, so he shouldn't be concerned, shouldn't be watching what she was doing the whole damn time. Worrying until it ate a hole in his gut.

But he couldn't stop himself.

'That reminds me,' Pete continued at the end of the line, 'I asked Marcy about those pains Colleen's been having and she said it was more than likely Braxton Hicks. False labour of sorts. Some women get them; some don't.'

'Yeah.' Eamonn nodded. 'The doc mentioned that, so I looked it up.'

'You and your darn research. You always were one for a project.'

'She's not a project.'

'Okay, so what *is* she, then?'

There it was. The million-dollar question. He had spoken to Pete on the phone almost every day since dropping the bombshell that he wasn't going to be back for a while. And in every conversation Pete had asked questions about Colleen. Just one or two in each call, but enough for him to have a fairly good idea of the overall picture, and a working knowledge of what had happened to her before Eamonn came home.

It had only been a matter of time before the questions became more Eamonn-focused.

He sighed again. *What was she?*

'She's Colleen. She's family, Pete.' He paused as he watched her move around the tail-end of the horse, knowing his initial answer was simplistic at best. It didn't come close to describing what she was. 'She's stubborn, feisty, and doing pretty damn well coping with everything she's been through. And I like to think we're friends now. That's all.'

But even that wasn't close, and Pete apparently knew him well enough to sense that from thousands of miles away. He probably knew it would take more than that to get Eamonn to stay in one place so willingly. Particularly a place he had left so far behind,

'Is it, now?'

The question raised a scowl. 'What do you want me to say?'

'Well, you could start with admitting that there's a tad more to it than her being family. That would be something. Because she's *not* family. And I don't recall you ever having a woman as a *friend*. So there's got to be something more. If you've even got round to admitting that to yourself, that is.'

He hadn't. But Pete's words made him stop and think. That had always been part of Pete's remit—to play the devil's advocate, to make Eamonn slow down and think. Up until fairly recently that friendship had taught him to stand back and look at things carefully, honestly. To see things from all angles.

It had taken being around Colleen for him to forget that training.

She just... Well, she just got under his skin. She confused things.

Eamonn had always been the kind of man who, when the wind blew him a particular direction, then that was where he went. Having fully investigated his destination, of course.

But *Colleen*—Colleen knocked him off-course. So that he couldn't see what was ahead and had to follow his gut instincts. It was exhilarating, in a way.

Maybe simply because she was the first woman he'd ever been impressed by. She made him want to do more, be more, give more. And it was the first time in his life he had felt driven to impress someone else, to try and raise himself to their level of strength and determination.

Yes, he'd always wanted to be successful at what he did— to prove that he could make something of himself even while he carried the guilt of shattering his father's dreams for him. And he'd succeeded. But this was different.

This time he wasn't trying to prove a point or build a

fortune. He was just trying to be a better person. To put someone else's welfare before his own.

But to what end? Where could it take him? What would be the point, beyond trying to make himself feel better when he left this time than he had the last?

'You still there?' Pete's voice sounded in his ear. 'Or are you doing some thinking?'

'Shut up, Pete.'

There was a burst of laughter. 'She's getting to you. *Man*, I gotta meet this one.'

'Goodbye, Pete.'

More laughter. 'Well, it happens to us all at some point. You've done well to escape it this long—'

'I'm hanging up now.' He leaned his head down and slowly lifted the receiver from his ear.

'You just let me know when to book time off for the wedding—'

'Hanging up. Bye, Pete. Love to Marcy.' He spoke the words louder as he reached the receiver all the way out to arm's length, and then hit the button to end the call, a smile on his face. Shaking his head, he set it down on the counter-top and looked back out of the window.

Wedding? *Like hell.* She might have him a little sideways, but she didn't have him pinned down. It was a bad case of curiosity, and maybe even a little jealousy at her ability to be so determined after adversity. That was all.

He watched for a few moments as she led the horse away and brought another one out to groom. Then he shook his head and went out to join her.

Just because he felt like it, and for no deeper reason than that.

'So much for you taking it easy. What do I have to do? Pin you down?'

She didn't turn to look at him, but he could see her smile as he got to her side. She continued to smooth the brush down the horse's neck. 'This *is* taking it easy. It's therapeutic.'

'Oh, is it, indeed?'

The hint of amusement in his voice made her turn her head, and she looked up at him with her blue eyes sparkling. 'You should give it a go.' Her smile grew as she held out the brush. 'Go on. *I dare you.*'

He looked down at her sparkling eyes for a long moment, smiling back. It was something he did a lot of in her company of late. And not necessarily because he found her unusually amusing. Though she could be that too.

'You're avoiding going to lie down for a rest by challenging me, aren't you, Colleen? I'm no fool, you know.'

She tilted her chin and quirked a finely arched brow at him. 'And *you're* avoiding a challenge because of the big scary horse, aren't you, Eamonn? I'm not dumb either.'

'*No*, ma'am. That you most certainly aren't.'

Colleen laughed when he made his American accent more pronounced, reaching down to lift his hand before she slapped the brush into it. 'Go on, then.'

The brush felt strange in his hand after so long. But he still remembered how to use it. Just because he had never actually loved the animals the way his father had, the way Colleen did, it didn't mean he was scared of them. Grooming one wasn't that big a deal.

But after her teasing he couldn't resist getting his own back.

So he looked down at it, turned it over, hid a smile, and stepped closer to the horse. Then he half-heartedly swept it over the animal's wide neck.

'*Wimp.*' Her voice sounded close to his shoulder. 'Not like that—like this.'

With her shoulder bumping against his forearm, she reached out a hand and laid it over his, against the horse's neck. Her fingers curled over his, her thumb circling round to touch the beating pulse on his wrist, and then she guided him, smoothed the brush down over the already sleek hair. 'Smooth, but firm. Yes, that's it.' She smiled in satisfaction, eyes focused on their hands as her voice melted into his eardrums. 'Then, at the end of your stroke, just flick a little— up and off. Like this.'

Eamonn's mouth had gone dry. The words 'smooth but firm' had done it.

Her long lashes flickered as she glanced up at him from the corner of her eye. Then she looked back at their hands, repeating the movement, smoothing the brush down, and at the end flicking up and off. Her throat convulsed as she swallowed.

'It's… Well, it's to encourage the horse's skin to produce oils to make the coat shine and help keep them waterproof. The…' She swallowed again. 'The little flick at the end helps remove any dust.'

When he finally found his voice it was low and husky. 'Yeah, I remember.'

Colleen's hand stilled, then she released his and stepped back, making space between them. 'Go on, then. Try it on your own.'

'Have you got a curry comb?' He smiled when she looked at him with suspicion. 'I need one to clean the body brush as I go along.'

Her eyes narrowed. She knew she'd been conned.

Laughter rumbled in his chest, worked its way up his

throat and burst free, circling them both as she glared at him with mock accusation.

'Why, you *rotten*—'

'Now, Colleen, be nice. I never said I didn't remember how to do it. You just assumed I didn't.'

'Well, *you* didn't correct me.'

His dimple flashed. 'No, I didn't, did I?'

It was fun, flirting with Colleen. He'd only managed to get past her prickly exterior enough these last few days even to try it. And at first he had told himself the only reason he was doing it was to tease her out of her funk.

Since they'd talked that early morning, after her revelations, something had changed in her. She was still feisty as be damned, and stubborn as all hell, but she had taken to watching him with a look of caution—and Eamonn didn't like that one little bit. So he'd decided, rather than go into another heavy emotional scene, that he'd tease her out of it.

Which was a *lot* more fun.

And, anyway, another emotional confrontation was the last thing she needed. He'd done his research.

With his Braxton Hicks research had come a wealth of information on things like high blood pressure and pre-eclampsia. Which Eamonn now knew was a *bad* thing.

By teasing her, laughing with her, flirting with her, he was encouraging her to relax around him. And keeping her blood pressure down.

Hooray for him. He was one helluva guy, really.

Because it had nothing at all to do with the fact that he loved hearing her lyrical laughter, loved it when her eyes sparkled up at him. Loved the fact that he smiled and laughed more in her presence than he had done in years.

But as she reached for a metal curry comb out of the

grooming box by the wall he saw her smile fade. Then she tensed. And, mid-bend to the box, she reached a hand across her midriff and grimaced.

Eamonn spun on her. Throwing the brush to one side, he reached out for her elbow. 'What's wrong? More Braxton Hicks?'

He had made her read all of his research as he'd found it. Tried to insist she understood why he was so keen to get her to relax. Even if at the time it had been his own method of justifying all he was doing to *help* her relax.

Colleen gasped, speaking to him through gritted teeth. 'I thought it was at the start. Now I'm not so sure.'

What?

He froze. 'What do you mean, at the *start*?'

Panting a couple of times, she blinked hard before she glanced up at him with a rueful smile. 'This has been happening all day, on and off.'

'On and off—*how often*?' The words were snapped out and his mouth thinned into a tense line. 'And how far apart, *exactly*?'

As the pain eased she straightened up, her face flushed as she looked him straight in the eye. 'Roughly.' She smiled. 'Oh, I'd have to say about every ten minutes.'

CHAPTER THIRTEEN

EAMONN leaned hard on the horn as a driver dared to think about pulling across into his lane. He swore viciously at him for trying.

In the passenger seat, Colleen smiled through the end of another painful contraction. 'It's hardly that poor man's fault, you know.'

'No, you're damn right it's not. *He* didn't wait 'til his contractions were ten minutes apart before telling anyone, *did he?*'

'I didn't know they were contractions at the start, and I already promised not to give birth in your rental car.'

'O-oh.' He laughed the word out with a burst of sarcastic laughter, aiming a quick, angry look in her direction that pinned her back further into her seat. 'You may not have known what they were at the start, Colleen McKenna, but after six-odd hours you can't tell me you didn't have a *damn good idea*! And you *know* how far away the hospital is from home. In case you don't, maybe I should just remind you. Forty miles. *Four-zero.'*

Her cheeks flamed as his voice rose on the last two words, and she frowned back at him in response. 'Well, maybe I read somewhere that first-time labours can take days, so I decided if I was really in labour then I could cut down on my time in the hospital.'

Eamonn lifted a hand from its vice-like grip on the steering wheel and waggled a finger at her. 'Don't you dare go using all that research I gave you as an excuse. That makes me partly to blame if you *do* give birth in this rental car, and I'm *not* having that kind of responsibility.'

'Well, if I do then I'll clean up any mess. Will that make you feel better?'

As the traffic came to a standstill again he glared over at her, his eyes skimming over the quirk of her brows, the challenge in her eyes and the stubborn tilt of her chin. His jaw clenched and unclenched. 'Don't you dare.'

He hid it well behind the glare, but Colleen was quick to notice the brief flash of panic in his eyes. She could chalk up that kind of intimacy to days spent solely in his company, she supposed. But the fact it was there at all briefly amused her. *Men.*

'You're not the one giving birth, here. All *you* have to do is drive.' Her mouth quirked at the edges.

He tilted his head in a sarcastic angle in answer. 'Well, y'know, I *would*. But someone chose to go into the final stages of labour in the middle of *rush hour traffic!*'

Her burst of laughter was cut off by another agonising wave of pain. She moaned, leaning forward and gripping the sides of the seat. *'Oh, God.'*

Eamonn swore again.

Colleen moaned again.

He glanced from her to the traffic lights and then reached a hand out for hers, unclenching her fingers from the side of the seat and wrapping them in his. Then he leaned closer, his voice dropping to a soft rumble. 'Hang on, darlin', hang on. We're nearly there. Breathe.'

When would he stop being nice to her when she needed it most? Was he *ever* going to stop being so thoughtful and considerate? *Damn him!*

She glared up into his eyes, teeth clenched hard as she growled, 'I *am* breathing. If I go blue you'll know I've stopped!'

His voice stayed soft, a tortured look on his face. 'I know it hurts—'

'Oh-you-*so*-don't!' Her fingers closed round his in a vice-like grip as she fought to keep from screaming. 'You have *no* idea!'

The lights changed and he pried his fingers from hers, over-revving the engine as he got them moving again. 'We're nearly there.'

'You're not kidding.'

It took the longest ten minutes of her life for them to finally reach the hospital, and then Eamonn was out of the car and opening the passenger door before she had time to recover from another contraction. When she tried to slap away his helping hands he scowled at her again, his voice rising. 'Let me help! We're here now, but we still have to get you to the maternity wing.'

'I don't *want* your help.'

'Yeah, you do. And even if you don't, you're getting it.' He had one of her hands trapped in his again, his other in the small of her back as he walked them across the car park.

And she hated him in that moment. Hated him for being right. Hated him for being so concerned. Hated him most of all for not being the father so he would have a real right to being all those things. She should have punished him by giving birth in the flipping car!

If it hadn't been for the thought of the pain-reducing drugs available to her mere feet away she would have done. Just to get back at him for breaking another little piece of her heart. Lord, if he'd been this baby's father then her child would never have wanted for anything, would it? He was just the type of man who would be there, who would offer support and protection and a hand to hold onto when it was needed. It just wasn't fair!

By the time they approached the reception desk to check in she was holding onto his hand like a lifeline. As if she could take on some of his strength by osmosis, to help her through what was yet to come. And she needed that strength. She was suddenly petrified beyond belief.

He nursed her through the check-in, settled her into the wheelchair that an orderly brought, kept his voice calm and soothing all the while.

By the time they were in the lift Colleen found herself crying silent tears. Because she knew she couldn't have got that far without him.

When Eamonn glanced down he saw them. And the sight gripped his chest, vice-like, breaking his heart in two. He was helpless again. Lost. What was happening to her was beyond his control, and that killed him. If there had been any way to save her the agony, to make things easier...

He hesitated for only a split second as the lift creaked up through the floors, then took a hand off the handles of the wheelchair, reaching for her. As if by touching her he could take some of her agony away.

When he touched the side of her neck, his fingertips caressing her jawline, she relaxed, her shoulders dropping down. Then she leaned her face into his touch, smoothed her cheek along the backs of his fingers while she reached up and placed her hand over his.

And they stayed that way in silence, until the lift stopped and the doors slid open.

Moments later a nurse and a midwife took the chair from Eamonn and turned it round, to wheel Colleen backwards towards swinging doors, towards the delivery room.

One of them smiled encouragingly at Eamonn. 'We can get you sorted out with a gown for the delivery room. Just give us a minute to get her settled.'

Eamonn and Colleen both swung their heads to face her with equally wide eyes, answering in unison.

'I'm not actually—'

'Oh, he's not coming in—'

They looked at each other and smiled.

The nurse smiled in return. 'Oh, well. Never worry, then. We always like to ask. But not everyone wants to come in. There's a waiting room down the hall to the left. Someone will come and tell you when it's over.'

But Eamonn wasn't watching her directions. He was looking at Colleen. The doors swung open behind her as they continued wheeling her away, and his chest cramped painfully, breathing became difficult.

She looked up into his face, searched his eyes with twin pools of summer-sky-blue, and smiled a watery smile.

Eamonn's throat closed, his voice a gruff whisper when he spoke. 'I'll be right here.'

Colleen couldn't seem to speak either. She nodded silently, blinking back her tears.

He took a step forwards as the nurse wheeled her further away. 'You'll be fine, darlin'. You know you will.'

Swallowing hard, she nodded again, then tried opening her mouth to speak and found she couldn't. So she did the next best thing and mouthed a silent *Thank you.*

And as the swinging doors closed, obscuring him from her view, she knew she didn't just mean for bringing her to the hospital in time.

'Mr McKenna?'

Eamonn was staring out through the blinds and into the middle distance, his mind a million miles away. Or just down the hallway, to be more precise.

He had honestly expected that because she had cut it so close there wouldn't be that long a wait. But he'd been there for hours. And the longer he waited, the worse he felt. The four nurses he had asked so far had all said she was fine. But what if something was wrong? What if there were complications and he hadn't got her here on time?

If anything happened to Colleen or her baby he would never, ever forgive himself...

'Mr McKenna?' The hand on his arm brought him out of his dark thoughts with a jolt, and he stared down at it in surprise, his brain not registering that he'd been called by the wrong name.

Slowly his eyes rose to the face of a girl in a nurse's uniform who didn't look old enough to be qualified. He blinked blindly at her, suddenly exhausted beyond words. 'Colleen?'

It was the only thought he had.

The nurse smiled. 'She's fine. Sleeping now. It was a tough birth.'

The hand on his arm moved to his elbow, and in a zombie-like state he allowed himself to be guided from the waiting room and along a corridor, while the girl prattled away at his side.

'Quite a large baby in the end. And stubborn about coming out, the midwife said. But they're both grand, so you don't need to worry. I'd say your wife will sleep for hours, though. I know I would.'

Eamonn was still working his way through 'tough birth' and 'large baby' while she led him through a doorway. So the words 'your wife' didn't register until she had let go of his arm and stepped forwards.

With a shake of his head to dislodge him from a surreal world, he opened his mouth to correct the mistake. And was stunned into silence again as she turned round.

In her arms was a bundle of blankets. Pink blankets. She stepped towards him, holding the baby out for him to take, her voice soft. 'She's just gorgeous, isn't she?'

Eamonn had held babies before. Well, he'd held Pete's babies—both of them. Had had them thrust into his arms unwillingly by a delighted father who had informed him it would be *good practice for when his time came*. So he knew how to hold her, how to support her head as he brought her safely against his chest. To where his heart thudded loudly and erratically.

What he didn't know was how it would *feel*.

Because in the instant she made contact with his chest she blinked and opened her eyes. Perfect, startling blue eyes, exactly like her mother's.

Everything stopped. His breathing. His heart.

When it beat again, he exhaled and smiled. 'Hello.'

She blinked up at him, moved her tiny mouth, and showed him the end of her pink tongue. Eamonn laughed softly.

It was the most perfectly magical moment he had ever experienced. He was holding Colleen's baby.

A death had brought him home. And now he was holding a new life in his arms. The cycle of life in a microcosm.

The nurse reached a finger out and gently pushed the blanket back from the edge of the tiny face. The woman smiled, looked up at Eamonn's face, and then back down again. 'She has a look of you about her, all right. Around the mouth especially. Congratulations.'

While he continued to blink down, mesmerised by the tiny face, the nurse patted his forearm and added, 'I'll be back in a few minutes. Give you two some time to get to know each other. If your wife is awake I'll come back and get you both. But I doubt she's stirred, to be honest.'

As she walked away Eamonn felt a pang of guilt for not correcting her. He should have. It was an easy enough mistake for her to have made. But he *wasn't* this gorgeous baby's father. Even if, for a brief moment, he wished he was.

But he knew, as she continued to blink up at him, that as long as he lived he would always be there for her. If she needed something he'd make sure she got it. If she needed help he'd be on the next plane. He didn't know why he felt that way, but he didn't *want* to know why. It was there, and that was that. Whether her mother approved or not.

While he was explaining that to the baby, in a low, husky voice, the nurse reappeared.

'Lord, I'm sorry. She *is* awake. And she wants to see the baby. So I said I'd bring you both in.'

'Can I carry her?'

The nurse smiled back. 'Well, we're not supposed to let you. They're supposed to go in the crib.' She backed down when he smiled a winning smile at her, dropping her voice to a conspiratorial whisper. 'But it's only a couple of doors down.'

Colleen was exhausted, emotionally and physically. She'd never felt so drained before. It was what she would cite as the cause for yet more tears when she looked back on the moment when Eamonn carried her daughter into the room. Reawakening her teenage dreams in a single heartbeat.

He stood in the doorway with her baby held in his arms and he smiled across at her, his eyes shining. It was both the most beautiful and the most heartbreaking thing Colleen had ever seen.

If only...

'Hello, Mummy.' His voice was husky as he walked to her bedside, his eyes flickering over her face. 'I found this baby in the hall and I thought you might like her.'

Colleen managed a smile through her moist eyes. 'The stork didn't drop her off. I can assure you of that.'

Eamonn leaned in closer and gently set her daughter in her waiting arms. Then he sat on the edge of the bed, facing them both, his fingers edging the blanket back so he could still see the tiny face.

Colleen waited to make sure she had her baby comfortable and safe before glancing up at his face again. He was staring down at the baby with such a look of amazement—of reverence, almost. When his eyes flickered up to meet hers and he smiled again she saw even more.

And Colleen couldn't help it. It was just too much. While she stared back down at her baby, overwhelmed with the bond she felt with her, she was also deeply conscious of the long finger on the blanket, of the man who looked down on her daughter with equally shining eyes.

When he looked up at her face again, she raised her eyes and blinked back the tears. But there were too many this time. It was just too damn much.

It was even more soul-destroying when he lifted his other hand to brush the tears off her cheeks with the end of his thumb, before snaking his fingers around her neck, into her hair, and drawing her head closer to place a lingering kiss on her forehead.

Then he leaned his own forehead against hers and looked into her eyes, up close. 'You're amazing.'

Colleen swallowed hard and squeaked out, 'No, I'm not.' She sniffed. 'Millions of women have babies every day.'

'None of them are you, though.'

Oh, this had to stop. It truly did. She was too weak to fight him off—or to fight with him. And now she had another poignant memory to add to her mental scrapbook for after he'd left.

So she leaned away from him and bowed her head to look down at her baby. That at least she could get right; she would shower her beautiful child with all the loving care she would ever need. Because even though she had worried while she was carrying her, about if she would be enough on her own, she now knew with complete certainty that she would be.

Even if she hadn't managed to give her a father who would look at her like Eamonn Murphy did.

This child would never suffer for the mistakes her mother had made before she was born. It was a new beginning. It *had* to be.

'What are you going to call her?'

'Evelyn.' She smiled, and wiped her cheeks with the back of a hand. 'It means "life".'

'It's perfect.' Eamonn nodded in approval in front of her. *'She's* perfect.'

Colleen took a deep breath. It was the first day of the rest of her life after all. The rest of *their* lives, hers and Evelyn's.

And the first thing she was going to do was take steps to let Eamonn know she was all right now. He didn't need to stay any longer.

So she pinned a smile onto her face and looked up at the crown of dark curls while he stared down at her baby. 'You must be wrecked.'

He glanced up and smiled a smile that melted her resolve. For a few seconds.

'A little, yeah. Not as much as you are, though.'

'You should head on back.' She nodded encouragingly, 'We'll be fine now. Thanks, Eamonn.'

The light in his hazel eyes faded in front of her gaze. He looked hurt for an instant. But that couldn't be right. What had *he* to be hurt about? She wasn't rejecting him. Because in order to make him feel rejected he'd have to care beyond the level of mild friendship, or business partnership. Which was all they had.

But she added a little more anyway. 'You've been great. I won't ever forget what you did for us.'

His eyes narrowed a barely perceivable amount. Then he looked down at Evelyn one more time. 'You're welcome. You both are.'

Colleen kept her smile in place as he stood up, watched as he glanced around the room and then back at her face. She even managed to keep smiling when a small frown appeared between his eyes.

Then he spoke in a different voice. A coolly polite voice. 'I'll see you in the morning, then.'

'I'll probably sleep half the morning away.'

'Then I'll be here after lunch.' His eyes swept over her face again, glanced down at Evelyn where she lay sleeping, and then over his shoulder to the door before he added, 'Call me if you need me to bring anything.'

And then he was gone. Little knowing he was taking a good chunk of Colleen's heart with him.

If only...

CHAPTER FOURTEEN

IT WAS a few days before the hospital let Eamonn bring them home. And then several days of meeting briefly in the kitchen or the hallway while Colleen adjusted to her new baby time-table. And a couple more on top of that before she became human enough to appear for regular lunch and dinner times.

By then Eamonn was getting more than a little frustrated with her attitude towards him.

He'd been patient to begin with, knowing he had to give her some time. She'd just had a baby. And if there was any more of a life-changing experience then Eamonn sure as hell couldn't think of it. It was bound to mean adjustments, inner doubts, stark terror. And she was bound to be physically tender, mentally drained, dog-tired.

So he'd worked round her, done more on the yard so she had one less thing to worry about. He'd taken care of the little things. Which only frustrated him further, because he wanted to do so much for her. But what he did had to be enough in the meantime—because she wouldn't let him do anything more.

After ten days he couldn't take it any more. His frustra-tion gave way to a simmering, festering anger. Because he really had no idea what it was he was doing wrong. What it was that had made Colleen close a hypothetical door on him and shut him out. And not just out of her life, but out of Evelyn's too.

It was doing his head in.

Oh, Colleen was polite. Polite as polite could be. She said *please* and *thank you* and basically closed him out of any deeper conversation at every opportunity she got. Though she did that politely as well.

She politely asked how the planning application was going, politely discussed what needed to be done in the yard, politely sent instructions for the yard girls.

She even discussed the weather from time to time. In a polite, talking-to-a-complete-stranger kind of way.

But she wouldn't enter into any intimate conversation— wouldn't stay in a room alone with him for any longer than five or ten minutes. Wouldn't let him even so much as stand and coo over Evelyn before she whisked her away to another part of the house.

Any hint of the blossoming friendship he'd thought they had before Evelyn's birth seemed like a figment of his imagination as time went on. And he missed it. He missed her laughter, the stubborn tilt to her chin when he would tease her or argue with her. He missed how they had begun to talk a little. And, no matter how he tried telling himself it shouldn't matter a damn, it did.

So, by the end of her second week home, Eamonn had had it with being patient. Especially when he found her falling asleep over her lunch at the kitchen table,

'You should try and catch some sleep while Evie is down.' He stood on the far side of the room and watched her reaction with cautious, hooded eyes.

Colleen pushed a hand back through her hair, blinking

long lashes as she tried to focus. 'I have a ton of stuff to do, and if she wakes up—'

'Then *I* can go get her.'

Her eyes narrowed the smallest amount while she thought, and even though it only took a few brief seconds Eamonn caught it. So he was scowling when she spoke. 'No, it's fine—really. I'll look after her. At least while I'm doing paperwork I'm within earshot.'

'I won't break her, you know.' He threw reason in first. It was bound to be a natural concern with a first-time mother after all.

'I know that.'

He followed reason with justification. 'And, despite what you might think, I know my way around a baby. Pete has two that I'm godfather to, so I know what to do.'

Her eyes rose, her lips parting as another polite answer made it out into the world. 'Thank you. I do appreciate that. But I'm fine, really. We just need to get into a routine, that's all.'

Eamonn stared her down, folding his arms across his chest and tilting his head slightly as his patience dwindled. 'And I'm sure you'll manage that when you eventually fall into an exhausted heap and can't hear her.'

There was a long pause, then, 'I sleep at night. I can look after my own child.'

'Ah, but you don't sleep at night, do you? She cried—what?—four times last night? Which means you're barely getting a couple of hours each time. And I know you're still sore. You can't tell me you're not. You *need* to get some sleep.'

The smile she aimed his way was clipped, nauseatingly polite, *false*; because it didn't make it all the way up into her eyes. 'I appreciate your concern, but—'

'Stop being so damn polite, would you?' He pushed off the counter as she slowly stood up to clear away her uneaten food with a tight-lipped expression that told him he was right about her still being sore. 'You want to try telling me exactly what it is I've done?'

Not looking at him, she moved around the kitchen—emptying her plate, rinsing it under the tap, setting it on the drainer—and all the while she was fighting to keep calm. It was killing her. But she really had no choice. If she didn't focus on being polite, on holding herself together, then she would fall apart at the seams. She was just so very tired. And it wasn't just from looking after Evelyn. A big part of her exhausted state came from being so on edge all the time, from always being aware of where Eamonn was, of the way he moved, the way he would look at her. She just felt she had to be a safe distance from him, keeping things cool. Not rocking the boat, so to speak.

'You haven't done anything wrong. Don't be silly.' Summoning up a last burst of energy, she turned her face in his direction and pinned a smile in place. It took an effort, and not just because she was so very tired, and living inside a body that felt completely alien to her. No, it had much more to do with the way Eamonn was looking at her again—the same way he had been doing so often of late.

With his hazel eyes narrowed, his mouth a tight line, and everything in his stance speaking of a dogged determination to make her talk to him.

But since he had walked into her hospital room holding Evelyn Colleen had been noticing way more than she was prepared to deal with. Not just about Eamonn, but about how being around Eamonn made her feel. And it was the latter that made her nervous.

Maybe it was partly some kind of genetic thing in new mothers—a built-in radar that made her more aware of everything in the vicinity of her child, so that every one of her senses were heightened. In olden days it had probably been to guard against predators…

As he stepped towards her, stood within inches of her body, Colleen realised that was probably still the case. Dramatic, yet true.

'What's going on?'

She tucked her hair behind her ear. 'Nothing's going on.' Her mind sought desperately for a reasonable explanation while one of her keenly aware senses overwhelmed her with his scent— hints of a spicy musk, and soap, and…him. She swallowed. 'Maybe I am just a little tired. But really there's nothing—'

'Oh, yes, there is. And I already know you're more than a *little* tired. So why won't you let me help?'

She swallowed again, unable to hold his steady gaze. Instead her eyes dropped to the base of his neck, above the shallow vee of his sweater, where she could see a hint of dark hair she hadn't noticed before, where a pulse was beating that she'd never been close enough to see before.

Before she had been large with Evelyn. And even though her body still hadn't completely recovered its pre-Evelyn shape, she was getting nearer to it—which meant his body was closer to hers than it had ever been. Which made holding herself together and concentrating on putting distance between them tougher than it had ever been.

It took breasts that were tight and aching and the dull ache below to remind her that she was in no physical shape either to do anything about her heightened awareness of him or, on the flipside, to have enough strength to physically fight him off.

So she had no choice but to talk to him. 'I just need to do things on my own, that's all. I can't rely on your help for ever, because that would be—'

'Trusting in someone again? Believing I'm capable of being a friend to you?'

She scowled at the husky edge to his voice that suddenly made their conversation more intimate. Intimacy of any kind was exactly what she was trying so hard to avoid. 'It's not a case of trust—'

'What is it, then? Is it that you're frightened that I won't look out for Evie properly?'

'*Evelyn.*' Her eyes shot up to clash with his, her anger rising. 'Her name is Evelyn. And if you'd flipping well stop interrupting me all the time I might actually be able to talk to you!'

The tight line of his mouth curved into a smile. But it wasn't one of the soft, almost affectionate smiles that he had aimed at her so often before she'd had Evelyn. It was a half-patronising/half-sarcastic smile that made her anger rise even further.

'Because you've been so *very* keen of late to talk to me, haven't you?' he said.

'Stop that!' Unconsciously her lips parted, and she ran the pink tip of her tongue across them before speaking again. 'I've been talking to you plenty of late, and you know I have. We've talked about planning, and the yard, and—'

'Everything except what it is that's been bugging you since you came home from hospital.'

Colleen stamped her foot on the tiled floor in frustration. 'Stop interrupting me! You've been doing it for weeks now, and *that's* something that really *bugs* me!'

'Is it, now?' The words were clipped out as he closed the final couple of inches between their bodies, pressing her back against the sink-edge without using his hands. In fact, he was barely touching her at all.

Because he knew she was still sore, still tender from

bringing Evelyn into the world. And, even while he was angry with her, he still thought to be considerate.

Which was worse. Because Colleen felt surrounded by him, overpowered by him, overwhelmed by his sensitivity to her needs that spoke of thoughtfulness and caring.

Her taut, aching breasts rose and fell in shuddering breaths as her pulse rose. Her heart thundered in her ears so that she was surprised by the sound of her own voice when she spoke.

'What else would it be?' Where had that sensual edge come from? Why had her anger translated into a husky edge that screamed of frustration and, Lord help her, desire?

It was as if holding everything back from him had made her want more, in some perverse way. Even when her body really wasn't capable of more. Not yet anyway.

Lifting her hands in defence, she laid her palms on the wide wall of his chest and pushed—*hard*. It was her first mistake.

Because his hands rose and trapped hers, his feet spreading further apart to balance himself so that her push didn't budge him an inch. Long fingers swept over the backs of her hands, lifted them, entwined with her smaller fingers, before placing their joined hands back onto his chest. Then his head tilted forwards and to one side, so that when he spoke his hot breath fanned across her cheeks and fluttered her eyelashes.

'It might just be that you're angry at me for something else, so you're trying to push me away. And you don't want to push me away. So you're fighting with *yourself*. And that's making you even angrier.'

The fact that he was pretty much on the mark fuelled her anger further. So she stood up onto her tiptoes, her face even closer to his, as she almost spat out, 'Or it might just be that I'm angry at you because you keep trying to ride roughshod over me. Because you have to be in charge. You have to be the dominant one because you're the man and I'm the woman. Maybe because that's your way of dealing with all the stuff that happened when you weren't here. You had no control over all the things that happened before, so you're over-compensating by being in charge of everything now.'

The gold in his eyes blazed at her words. It should have been a warning sign for Colleen, but she kept going regardless. Her second mistake. 'But if that's some subconscious way of punishing me even when you claimed you understood—'

Eamonn shut her up the only way he could. In an instant he rocked back, tugging on her hands so that her body swung into his. Then, as she gasped in surprise, he dropped his mouth onto hers and pushed her back so that she was pinned in place between his hard body and the cold sink-edge.

Their first kiss had been soft, sweet. The memory of it lingered in the back of his mind even while it registered that this kiss was a different story altogether.

This one might have been born of anger, but it spoke much more of frustration. At least on his part. Ever since he'd come home she'd been burrowing under his skin, occupying his thoughts, twisting him up. When he'd held her baby for the first and only time he'd felt connected to Colleen in a way he'd never been connected to another woman. As if, in some small way, Evie had become partly his because he was entangled with her mother.

To then be shut out, held at arm's length, treated with a bitter pill of politeness…

It had made him insane.

He made Colleen pay for that in the first few moments of this kiss. Using only his lips as punishment, he moved his mouth over hers in swift, hard strokes, not seeking, but *de-*

manding that she give in. That she stopped fighting and surrendered to him.

For a moment she froze, just let him take, allowed him to make his demands without making so much as a whimper in protest or even breathing. But when he lifted his mouth to change the angle she raised her chin and found him again, matching him touch for touch, stroke for stroke. It was all it took for him to slow down, to make the kiss more than just a form of punishment.

So the tempo changed. And it was only then that Eamonn released her hands and wrapped his arms around her body, holding her gently within his grasp as their ragged breathing filled the silent room. He ran his tongue along the same path hers had followed while they argued, and she opened for him, met him halfway, and they danced.

But when he ran his hands over her back, smoothed under the edge of her voluminous T-shirt and touched her skin, she gasped again and froze.

Eamonn knew that without thinking he had pushed too far, too fast. He didn't want to hurt her, knew it was too soon to make a demand on her body. No matter what his own body wanted right at that moment. And he swore inwardly at his own stupidity.

'Stop.' She said the word against his lips, tilting her head back, eyes still closed while she prayed that he would. Because if he continued she wasn't sure she had the strength to stop him kissing her again. And no amount of heartfelt need could compensate for the fragility of her body. As it had for most of her life, her sense of timing continued to suck. Bigtime.

He stopped. Let his fingertips whisper down over the soft skin on her back, then stepped back from her. Just the one step, while he watched her face and waited for her eyes to open. It was the longest wait in his life. He wanted the right to hold onto her, to soothe her with his voice, his lips and his touch, until she softened and trusted in him. Let him back in through the doorway she had closed.

There was nothing he remembered ever wanting more.

His eyes moved over the long lashes against her flushed cheeks, her swollen lips, the shaky rise and fall of her lush, full breasts. Until finally he couldn't stand it any more.

'Colleen—'

'No.' Her eyes opened, fixed on his. 'No. This time I'm the one interrupting. Because there's no point to this, and you know that as well as I do. It's not like this is going anywhere. Even if my body *was* up to it, which it's not.'

Eamonn frowned at her reasoning.

But with another deep breath she continued. 'There's no point in me getting used to you being here, in learning to lean on you, or trust that you'll take the weight when I need you to. Or…or *anything* else.'

Her hesitation before the 'anything else' brought a hint of a smile to his eyes. The very fact that she'd hesitated, that her words had been said on such a husky tone, that she'd had to take so many deep breaths to stay in control, all pointed to the one thing he wanted to see.

Because, as much as the impulse to kiss her had caught him off-guard, there was something between them. And she was feeling it too. All the signs were there. It wasn't as if Eamonn was some adolescent kid who couldn't read the signs of basic physical awareness between a man and a woman, now, was it?

Lifting one hand again, he touched it against her side, smoothed it up from her hip to press the material of her shirt into the curve of her waist.

She jerked away from the touch, as if he'd burned her, her breath hitching as the flush on her cheeks deepened. 'Please don't. I'm really not in any shape for you to be touching me.'

'But it's not that you don't *want* me to touch you.'

Her lashes flickered down to his chest and a frown appeared between her arched brows. Another breath, and then she looked up. 'Sometimes people can want something even when they know it's not good for them. If there's one thing I've learned this past year, it's self-preservation. You won't stay here, Eamonn. We both know that. Your life is an ocean away. And I'm not the kind of girl who can just fill in some time. So this stops here. It stops now. It has to.'

There was barely a heartbeat of a pause before Eamonn asked, 'And what if I *don't* go? What then?'

CHAPTER FIFTEEN

COLLEEN looked as stunned that he'd said the words as Eamonn felt at having said them.

'What do you mean, if you *don't* go? You're being ridiculous.' She laughed nervously. 'Of course you're going to go!'

He swallowed as he stared at her, her eyes wide and surprised. And for a moment he didn't honestly know what to say. It wasn't as if he'd sat down and had a long, contemplative think about putting down roots and staying, leaving his life in New York to settle down in the tiny place he'd come from.

With Colleen and her baby.

It was a serious, serious commitment. Something he'd never felt the urge to do before. And that kind of a commitment deserved a serious thought process. It didn't need to be blurted out as a way out of an argument.

His momentary silence gave him away.

Colleen laughed again, her hand pushing at the strand that was already tucked safely behind her ear while she avoided his gaze. 'You'll really say anything to win an argument with me, won't you? We both know you have a whole life, including a career you wanted more than anything else. And all of that's away from here.'

'I know that.'

Her eyes shot back to his face. What was he *doing*?

When she had thrown the words at him she had fully expected that he would move away from her, that he would back down. Because he had to see the truth in what she was saying. And, to be honest, if he hadn't gone and kissed her she would never even have brought it up. She would have just continued being polite, smiling when required. Until he left and she had to get on with the rest of her life.

Damage control. That had been the plan.

But the minute his mouth had settled on hers she had known the damage was already done. She was already lost. When she had given her heart to him as a naïve teenager it had been a drop in the ocean compared to the wave of differing emotions she now felt for him.

Maybe if he hadn't been so thoughtful and considerate since he'd come back. Maybe if he hadn't seemed to genuinely care about getting Inisfree back on its feet. Maybe if he'd been as angry with her at what had happened as she'd been with herself. Maybe if he hadn't held her in his arms and kissed her with a gentleness that had left her aching for something more. Maybe if he hadn't made her feel safe and protected while she was pregnant. Maybe if he hadn't carried her daughter in his arms.

Maybe then she wouldn't have fallen in love with him.

But if there was one thing Colleen had learnt in the last while, it was that she couldn't live her life on maybes any more. There was what *wasn't* there, and there was what *was*. Those were the simple facts of her life.

And the most pertinent fact was, no amount of damage

control could have protected her from something that had already happened. Had, in fact, had its seeds sown a decade and a half ago when he had shattered her heart by leaving.

As he would again. No matter what he said in the heat of the moment.

She shook her head, the errant lock working free to flick against her cheek. 'You hate it here. You could never be happy.'

'No, it's not that I ever hated it. I've told you that before. I just wanted something more.'

'And you have something more. In *New York*.'

'Which will still be there, regardless of where I decide to spend time. It's not like I haven't taken a break or two before now.'

Colleen's heart thundered. He couldn't be saying these things to her. She had to be imagining it. Her heart wanted it to be true so badly that her mind was misreading what he was saying.

He'd mentioned taking a break. That was all. No promises, no guarantees. And in taking a chance like that surely she'd be risking too much, no matter how much she wanted it?

Eamonn took a breath and stared at her with a steady gaze. 'I'll admit I haven't thought this through—'

'You're damn right you haven't thought this through. Good God, are women so thin on the ground in New York that one wee kiss or two has you packing your bags and upping sticks to live back here for a while in dear old Ireland? The place you left so fast your feet barely touched the ground!'

His eyes narrowed. 'Oh, there's a bit more to it than that, and we both know it.'

She laughed nervously. 'I know no such thing.'

'Yes.' The word was firm, his look implacable. 'You do. You think we haven't been heading towards something like this for a while now? You think I run around all over the world seeking pregnant women to look after? My father was already gone. There was nothing I could have done to change that, or the fact that I wasn't here to say goodbye. But I came anyway. I could have wrapped things up in a day. But I didn't—*did I?*'

'Only because you didn't know what you were walking into! You can't tell me that if you'd come back, this place had been working like clockwork and I hadn't been wandering around like some poor pregnant waif you wouldn't still have been gone inside a day.'

The description she'd used to describe herself brought a smile to his face. 'Oh, you were hardly some poor pregnant waif. You're one of the gutsiest women I've ever met.'

That was how little he knew. But before she could make some sarcastic retort in answer he had moved in again, his hands settling on the counter behind her so that she was trapped between the steel bands of his arms.

She looked from side to side, measuring up her chances of escape with a frown. If she could just put some distance between their bodies she might stand a chance of keeping her mind on making a more convincing stand.

When he spoke again, his face was closer, his voice a vibrating rumble that teased the air between them. 'You get to me. You've been getting to me since the day I arrived, and I can't give you a deep insight into why that is. It's just there. And your trying to shut me out like you have these last few days has been hell.'

'I wasn't trying to shut you out—'

'Sure you weren't.'

The frown was still in place as her lashes fluttered upwards and she risked another look into his eyes. 'I was trying to let you see that I was getting on with life. That there's nothing to hold you here any more.'

'You see now…' He lifted a hand and tucked back the curling strand of hair, his gaze lingering on it as he trapped it between his thumb and forefinger, smoothing down its silky length. Then he looked back into the sparkling blue of her eyes. 'That wouldn't be entirely true.'

'Don't you dare kiss me again.'

He smiled, the dimple in his cheek creasing. 'Are you daring me?'

'No. I'm telling you not to.' She raised her chin.

Which, whether she knew it or not, was an open invitation to do exactly what she was telling him not to do. But, exerting as much self-control as he'd ever had to, Eamonn merely let his finger slip off the end of the strand of hair. He trailed it from the soft skin behind her earlobe, down along her jaw, until he had it beneath her chin.

'You don't protest when I'm kissing you. You kiss me back.' Rubbing the pad of his thumb back and forth in the dip below her mouth, he watched with hooded eyes as her lips parted in response. 'Would it be so bad if we just gave it a shot? Saw where it took us?'

Where it took them? To heaven or to hell was where it could take *her*. What else was it for him, barring a way to fill in some time 'til he left again?

But to have her dream of old offered to her on a plate? It was the biggest temptation she'd ever had.

Consequently, despite her best efforts, her lower lip trembled before she answered in a low whisper, 'And what if it doesn't work? What then? You might be able to just get on a plane and forget about it, but I'd be left here. *Again*. I can't have my life here tainted with yet another mess.'

'We don't know it wouldn't work. I can give it a shot if you can.'

'We don't know that it *would* work. And taking a shot might make more of a mess than either of us want.'

'That's the chance that everyone takes, though, isn't it?' He smiled a devastatingly sensuous smile, his voice dropping to an intimate grumble. 'Leastways that's what I'm told. Big risks for big gains. I'm a gambler, Colleen. The question here is, are you?'

Colleen's eyes closed, a shudder passing over her body as she took a deep breath. When she looked at him again it was almost a look of anguish, and it tore Eamonn's heart.

'Even if it worked you would never be happy unless you were running off to Timbuktu or some place every few months. There's a world out there that you love seeing. I can't compete with that.'

Her hand rose, removing his thumb from her face, settling his arm back by his side. This time he let her do it. But he still didn't move away.

Even while his mind knew her words made perfect sense, he hated to lose an argument. So he continued looking for ways to prove her wrong.

'Maybe you could come with me? See those places with me. Broaden your horizons some.'

'With a baby in tow?' Colleen smiled sadly, slowly shaking her head from side to side. 'And even if she was old enough to travel, what would we do when she got to school age? If it even lasted that long? It just wouldn't work. I want my baby to know where she came from. I want her to know her roots and her heritage. If she decides she wants to see the world when she's grown, then that'll be her choice. I can't drag her from one place to another. It wouldn't be fair. Gambling doesn't really come into it when you're responsible for a child, Eamonn.'

Even as she said it, Eamonn knew he would feel the same way. To a certain extent. No matter how far he'd travelled, or where he'd decided to live, he'd always been Irish, felt Irish. It gave him a grounding, a history that went beyond his lifespan. And he would want that for Evie too. But admitting that meant conceding a point in a greater debate.

Could he give up that much of himself for Colleen? Could he stay and be happy? In asking her to try was he asking too much? Being too selfish?

He'd always been a man who grasped what he wanted, chased it down, held onto it. But he'd never wanted something so huge and life-changing before. Not on such an emotional level.

But if he didn't try he knew he'd spend the rest of his life wondering what would have happened if he did.

'We can talk about the travelling issue if it becomes a problem. But when it comes to leaving here, you'll have to tell me to go, Colleen. Because I'm staying put. I want us to try this. Won't you wonder what might have happened if we don't? I know I will.'

Colleen stared up at him. He had no idea what he was asking of her. Because, for her, every minute, hour and day that they spent together would make it more painful when he *did* leave. Which he would, wouldn't he?

At the same time, a minuscule part of her heart was asking what would happen if he didn't? What if the shaky foundation they already had—their shared legacy, a partly shared past—*was* enough to build on? It was almost too much to hope for. Could the precious dreams she'd once held so tightly in adolescence blossom into something real in adult-hood?

And wouldn't it be better to try while Evelyn was so small? Because to have such an important figure in her life as an older child would inevitably lead to a bond that would leave more than one broken heart if he ever walked away.

And he was right. She *would* wonder what might have happened. The question was, could she hold back enough of herself to survive if it didn't work?

Her confused thoughts must have shown on her face. Because with a flash of determination in his eyes he raised his hands again, framing her face. He let his thumbs touch the corners of her mouth, his pupils dilating as he focused on her lips. And when she didn't protest he leaned in for another kiss.

A firm kiss, a slow kiss. That stole the air from her lungs and breathed more hope into her heart. She couldn't fight him off when he kissed her. She really couldn't. Because her blood hummed through her veins, her knees wobbled, she even felt dizzy for a second. And in an instant she was more alive than she'd ever been.

How was she supposed to fight that?

And then, if that wasn't enough, he raised his mouth less than an inch from hers and whispered so low that she barely heard it, 'Let's just see what happens. Please?' He smiled *that* smile again. 'You know you want to.'

Please wasn't a word she'd heard him use too often. And when it was said in such a low tone, with the gold in his eyes flaming so close to hers that she heated up with just his look…

How was she supposed to keep on saying no?

Evelyn chose that moment to cry from the front room, the sound echoing through the house.

Eamonn raised his head, turned his face towards the sound. Then he looked at Colleen with the question in his eyes before he said it. 'Will you let me get her?'

It was her first test. The first signal that she was prepared to let him into her life. And they both knew it.

With a deep, shuddering breath she nodded.

He seemed to understand how big a step it was for her, what it meant. And his answering smile almost lit up the room in victory. Taking only the time it took to place a loud, smacking kiss on her lips, he released her and stepped away. 'We'll be right back. And then maybe you'll trust me with her enough to get some rest. I need you to get your strength back. *Soon.*'

Colleen didn't breathe again until he'd left the room. And then her heart beat nineteen to the dozen until he came back.

He needed her to get her strength back? *Soon?*

Her heart continued to thunder. Her breasts tingled. And she knew it wasn't just a biological response to her child being brought to her. Oh, no. She knew rightly what it was.

She knew from the gleam in his eyes what he had in mind for when she got her strength back.

What she had to do was shut off a little of her heart in the meantime. Learn to survive this time. No matter what happened.

CHAPTER SIXTEEN

'So who exactly is the hot guy in the yard?'

Colleen glanced out of the kitchen window to where Eamonn was giving instructions to the new handymen he had hired. The immaculate jeans he had brought with him had taken a hammering, as had many of his expensive shirts. But he didn't seem to give a damn. In fact, his enthusiasm for getting the place back in shape was boundless. And, of all the things he did or said, it was the one thing that gave her the most hope.

If she was right to hope at all. Because every glimmer of hope was breaking down her carefully erected barrier over that portion of her heart she was holding back from him. In order to survive.

With a breath she turned from the window to face her friend. So much had happened since Becky had taken her horses jumping on the mainland. She had a lot to catch up on, even without cooing over Evie.

'He's Declan's son.'

Becky's eyes widened. 'That's Eamonn Murphy? You're kidding! What's he doing here? I thought he lived in the States? Has he been here long?'

Colleen smiled at the deluge of questions. 'Yes, it is. No, I'm not kidding. He's staying for a while. Yes, he does live in the States—and just over seven weeks. Anything else you want to know?'

'Is he single?'

Now, *that* was a loaded question.

'He's not married, if that's what you mean.'

Becky's jaw dropped. 'Well, now.' She grinned. 'That *is* interesting.'

For a split second Colleen honestly hated her friend. Becky was in great shape. She'd been a professional show-jumper for years, and had the toned body to prove it. She was exactly the kind of girl Eamonn would have chased back in the day.

Folding her arms across her breasts, Colleen did what she'd wanted to do to all those girls years ago. She smiled a narrow-eyed smile and warned, 'You just keep your paws off him, you hear?'

Becky laughed aloud. 'It's all right. I got it when you said "If that's what you mean". You are so transparent. So, tell all…'

'There's nothing to tell.'

Which was a flat-out, bare-faced lie. There was too much to tell. And not enough time to tell it before Eamonn would appear for lunch.

And where would she begin?

Well, she could begin with the fact that she was in turns happier than she'd ever been in her entire life and more heart-broken than she'd ever been in her life. Every day she spent with him spun her around, made her feel both safe and in grave danger at the same time.

Her eyes moved to the window again as she heard his laughter echo over the yard. He seemed to take so much joy in improving the place, in working with her to build Inisfree into something even better than it had been before. And his enthusiasm made her love him all the more. Because he wasn't just taking care of business; he was lavishing love on the place she loved. If he could just care for it as much as she did then there was hope…

She smiled softly. There she was, hoping again.

'Wow! You've got it bad, haven't you?'

Her eyes were drawn back to her friend. 'Oh, yeah. But it's too early to pull it apart in a discussion with you.'

Becky shrugged. 'I can't help it if I'm protective.'

And Colleen appreciated that, she really did. Becky had been her shoulder to cry on before she'd headed off on the UK circuit, and she'd missed her. She had. But she really wasn't ready to discuss something that was still on such fragile ground.

'I'm fine this time, Becky—really.' With what she hoped was an encouraging smile, she drew a chair out at the table. 'Now, tell me some good news about your tour.'

Becky's face was illuminated as she leaned forwards over the table. 'Oh, I have good news. But it's not just for me.'

'And that means that Inisfree horses will go up in price?'

Colleen grinned up at him from where she had her head resting on the sofa-back, her eyes gleaming with enthusiasm. 'It will certainly help. Becky's mare has amassed plenty of points on the circuit, but if an international rider buys her for the Olympics and she does well then people will look at the breeding. And that puts us on the map.'

Eamonn nodded in understanding as he ran his hands along her jean-clad calves. Her legs were lying across his lap as they talked. 'Be a good time for a website, then.'

She tried to ignore the warmth that spread up her legs as he touched her. With the boundaries of physical contact more open, and yet still limited by her body's capabilities, it made every touch a thrill, a tease, a promise of things to come. So that talking about Inisfree-related topics was the best thing she had to help distract her from her rapidly rising frustration.

Eamonn seemed to be coping just fine with the lack of real physical contact. Which made her nervous. Why wasn't he as frustrated as she was? She knew she wasn't supermodel material, even when she was in shape. And while she still wasn't entirely comfortable within her own skin how could she hope to be attractive enough for him? She hated the fact she even thought that way—like a lesser woman, almost.

If she could just get back in shape then she would at least have her confidence back. And then she could give as good as she got.

But, although she was closer, it would still be a while before she regained her shape, was physically fit again. Was more *ready* to accommodate him than she already was.

If they could make love it would help bind him to her. And that, added to his caring about Inisfree, might just be enough. It might even help her believe their relationship wasn't a fragile thing that could be easily broken. Which was what she feared the most.

Maybe if she discussed it with him…

But where did she even begin with a conversation like that? She didn't want to be one of those women who had to dissect every segment of a relationship to make it work. She never had been before. But then, she'd never been in a relationship that mattered so much before.

Somewhere in her mind she was still convinced they were on borrowed time. Any day soon her shot at a dream might end. And then she'd have to face going on alone. Knowing she'd lost the one man she would always love more than any other. What man could possibly compare? Especially when the last one she'd chosen in Eamonn's shadow had been so very bad a choice.

Focusing on Inisfree was easier. The chicken's way out, maybe, but easier. And she still felt she had to encourage the enthusiasm he had for the place. It was a pro-active starting point, which meant she was doing something positive. Even if she still couldn't completely allow herself to believe.

'Sounds good.' She absent-mindedly toyed with the curls of hair that touched the collar of his shirt. 'As soon as we get the plots sorted and sold we could look into getting that done. Properly this time.'

Eamonn's eyes sparkled across at her in the dimly lit room. 'We don't need to wait. I'll get the guys in New York who did my company's web work to put a package together.'

'No, you're not spending any more of your own money. I thought we already agreed that?' Her hand stilled, but she smiled as she said it, trying to convey the fact that she wasn't being confrontational. 'This place has to stand on its own two feet. And if it can't then there's no point in you going broke trying to save it.'

'Actually, I don't think we *did* agree that. And there's nothing wrong with speculating to accumulate.'

'Only when the place can afford to speculate by itself.'

'So I can't invest in improving the value of something that's half mine?'

It was a good point. And not one Colleen had ever considered before. But then, in fairness, she'd never sat down and thought about how things would work if Eamonn decided to keep a vested interest in the place. The dream had always been that *she* would run it—it was her baby, always had been. And Declan had even helped groom her for that after Eamonn had left and her parents had died.

Finding a working relationship with Eamonn would be a real test for them both. Many a relationship fell apart because there were cracks that became voids when a couple lived *and* worked together. *If* they even survived that long.

There was so little to hold them together, and so much that could pull them apart.

With a small frown of concentration she dragged her eyes from his steady gaze and played with his hair again. 'There's no point if the place can do it itself in a couple of months. Let's just wait and see what happens.'

His hands stilled. 'We're not talking about the business now, are we?'

'Yes, we are.'

'Not entirely, we're not.' His deep voice remained steady as he stared at her face. 'You don't want me to invest in case you and me don't work out.'

There were times when Colleen really hated that he could read her so well. It was disconcerting. It meant she had to think on her feet all the time. And that was exhausting.

Somehow she managed to keep her voice calm. It was something she'd been working hard on since they'd come to their unsteady truce as they tentatively walked onto the grounds of a 'relationship'. Whatever *that* was.

'I think it would be better to keep things simple, for now. Surely that makes sense?'

'We don't stand a chance if you keep planning for the worst all the time. Doesn't *that* fact make any sense?'

Her gaze flickered to his, while she still tried to hold onto calmness. 'You think after the year I've had that it doesn't make sense for me to be cautious? If we tangle up the business with this then it makes it a bigger mess at the end.'

'And you're still determined there'll *be* an end?'

It was too much to hope otherwise. That was why. The odds were already against them.

Reluctantly dropping her hand from his thick hair, she pushed her body into a more upright position. Then she took a breath or two. 'All right, so maybe I will admit that I still have a few difficulties believing that there's enough here for you. Even though you've looked so happy on the yard these last few weeks. But your life in New York is bound to be more interesting than fixing a few fences here.'

'You don't know what my life in New York is like.'

She leaned a little closer, her head tilting in challenge. 'Only because you haven't told me much. But you still have to spend half the afternoon on the computer and the phone, so it's not that you're not kept busy, is it? It has to be more fulfilling for you than this place.'

Eamonn seemed to tense beside her, his thick lashes brushing against his skin as he looked down to where his hands lay on her legs. He swallowed as he thought, and Colleen watched the movement, still close to him physically but feeling a sudden gap between them. It sent a chill along her spine, wrapped icy fingers of dread around her heart.

He looked back up before he spoke. 'The only way I know of to get you to understand what New York is like for me is to show you. You could come over for a visit when I go back.'

Her eyes widened at 'when I go back'. The words were so very definite and final. He was already planning on when he was going back. So why were they even having this con-versation? Why were they doing this? Even while he was trying to convince her they could work through the bigger issues later on, he was feeding her fears—denying what he was trying to convince her of by subconsciously dropping hints into the conversation. As if he'd already looked ahead and planned to go away from where he was.

'I'll have to go back. If you come for a visit and it goes okay, then you could stay at my place.'

Leave her home? He knew better than that.

'Flying back and forth for wee visits would work out very expensive over time. And anyway, I'm a small-town kind of girl. I've never been anywhere worth talking about. This place is all the home I need.'

'You shouldn't narrow your horizons so much. There's a big world out there.'

'Maybe, but Evie—'

He lifted a large hand from her leg and used it to tilt her chin up. 'Don't do that.'

The softly spoken demand tugged at her heartstrings as surely as the brush of his fingers on her skin raised her pulse. But his eyes gave nothing away, and Colleen needed something more. She just didn't feel she could ask for it. As if her asking rather than his volunteering would somehow make his answer less truthful.

'Don't use Evie as something to hide behind. She's too little for that.'

'I'm not.'

'Yeah.' He nodded. 'You are. I'm trying here, Colleen. But you've got to meet me halfway at some point.'

Meet him halfway to what? Because there still weren't any words. Not words that spoke of deep feelings that would hold them together through all the other stuff. Not words that said he would stay, that she could trust him and rely on him. Completely. Without holding back.

And she wanted that. More than she'd ever wanted anything before. But enough to give up the one home she'd known for her entire life?

The phone rang in the other room and Eamonn's head turned towards the sound. He frowned. 'It's late. That has to be Pete.'

Colleen swung her legs round 'til her feet were on the floor. 'You better go get it.'

But he hesitated, leaning down to kiss her soundly before raising his head to warn her, 'We're not done here.'

'I know.'

The phone continued to ring. But Eamonn stayed where he was, his face inches from hers as he searched her eyes for answers. 'What do I have to do to get you to trust me?'

Love me as much as I love you.

That was all it would take. But to ask for it was something different. She couldn't make him feel something if it wasn't there. Wouldn't humiliate herself by doing so.

The phone rang and rang. The noise raised a cry from upstairs.

Which made Colleen smile wryly before she raised her hands and pushed against his shoulders. 'Go get the phone. I'll see to Evie.'

Eamonn frowned down at her for a long moment. Then he leaned back on his heels and glanced towards the door. A couple of steps away he hesitated again, turning to look at her as she stood up. 'I'm not going anywhere. I mean that. I'm just going to have to prove it by staying put 'til you *do* believe me. I've got time. And then we'll have a proper talk, you and me.'

But when he answered the phone Pete's words made a lie of his own. Drawing him from the surreal world of home and hearth back to reality.

'I need you back here, *pronto*. We got problems.'

CHAPTER SEVENTEEN

SHE was in the nursery when he went to look for her. For a moment he almost walked away. But his feet wouldn't move, so he stood in the doorway, transfixed.

Ever since he'd come home he'd been standing in doorways, looking in on Colleen. It had happened the day he'd arrived, the day he'd brought Evie to her in the hospital. And now it was happening again. While she breastfed her baby.

The response it evoked in him was more powerful, more primal than anything he'd ever felt before. If someone had ever told him that such a simple, natural act could conjure up so many different emotions he would never have believed them. But there he was, standing in a doorway, experiencing every emotion he had.

Had she any idea how beautiful she was? With her child in her arms, that tiny version of herself who had wormed her way into his heart the day he had first looked at her. In the same way Colleen had been doing since he'd first set eyes on her behind the huge desk in the yard office.

With Evie it had been an instantaneous thing. But the depth of feelings he was developing for Colleen was creeping up on him slowly. Slowly, but they were there.

Suddenly it felt as if he was looking in on the two people who mattered more to him than anything else. He wanted to take care of them, to keep them safe from any of the bad things that life might try and throw their way. He wanted to have Colleen by his side as they watched Evie smile for the first time, laugh for the first time, take her first steps. For the first time in his life he was tempted by the thought of being grounded, of having a place that wasn't just somewhere to live and fill in time between trips. Somewhere he could call home.

But what was home to him? It was the one answer that had evaded him for most of his life.

Maybe a part of it was how he had felt lately, building Inisfree back to its former glory. He wasn't just increasing the value of a business investment, he knew that. Had known it for weeks. He was helping build a home that Colleen and Evie could be proud of. But while he was doing it, and with all the satisfaction he was getting doing the manual work, he was also deeply aware that Colleen was the bigger challenge to him. And the bigger prize.

What could he do to convince her that what they already had was worth making compromises for? How could he convince her that he wanted to stay a while and see if they could make it work when he now had to tell her he had to leave?

While he stood looking in on her he felt completely lost, floundering in a sea of uncertainty. The one time when the right words were needed more than ever, and he couldn't find any. He couldn't just bound in there, interrupting such a perfect scene, and try to force her to feel something she didn't. Could he?

It would take time. And once he'd sorted out what needed sorting in New York he was going to clear the boards to make that time. No matter how long it took.

It would be worth the time and effort if it brought Colleen into his empty arms. If it got her to let down her final barriers and allow him completely into her life. It was as if gaining her trust in something so big would allow him to do the same in return.

Then her head rose and she looked straight at him. She didn't say a word. Didn't look outraged that he was standing watching something so intimate. She just blinked at him, breathing steadily.

Then she smiled an almost ethereal smile.

Eamonn walked into the room and hunched down beside her, looking up into the deep blue of her eyes for a long moment before he answered her smile with one of his own.

The sound of Evie suckling caught his ear, and he looked down to where her head was tucked tightly against Colleen's creamy breast. It was amazing. It was beautiful. He felt his chest tighten, he felt weaker than he'd ever felt before.

Could she see that she did that to him?

Another upward glance, hazel eyes locked with blue, and his hazel took in the widening of her dark pupils, the heat in her gaze. The fact that she looked at him like that, with such tenderness, made him feel triumphant—as if he was ten feet tall even while hunched down beside her.

Then he looked back down, and he couldn't stop himself. He reached out his index finger and smoothed back the edge of Colleen's shirt so he could see better.

Her breasts rose and fell in shallow breaths as he then smoothed his fingers over Evie's head, brushing the soft down of her baby hair into place.

He knew every strand of her almost white-blonde hair, knew how it felt to have her blink up at him with her amazing blue eyes, knew what the tightening in his chest was like when she closed a tiny fist around his index finger in a grip that spoke of a determination and strength that defied her size. He knew Evie because since Colleen had allowed him to spend time with her again he had been memorising Evie, not wanting to miss a thing.

But her mother remained as much of a mystery to be unravelled as she had been the day he'd come back.

Another upward glance, this time taking in the parting of her lips along the way, the faint tinge of warmth on her cheeks. Everything about her was tugging him in on invisible threads.

Evie continued to suckle while Eamonn's fingers moved in smooth strokes over her head, his eyes fixed on Colleen's.

It only took a slight rock forwards onto the balls of his feet and he was able to place his mouth on Colleen's in a feather-light kiss. Once, twice, before he nudged her nose with the end of his and smiled. When he spoke, his voice was a deep, rumbling whisper.

'How long did you say it would be 'til your body is recovered from having Evie?'

Colleen smiled a smile that spoke of feminine sexual empowerment. 'Not soon enough, as far as I'm concerned.'

His grumble of laughter washed over her face. 'Me either. But I need you to have the all-clear from the doctor. I don't want to hurt you.'

'I know.' The words were whispered back, as if she understood he didn't mean just physical hurt.

Something crossed over his eyes in response. 'I won't rush you into anything.'

Rush her? Colleen quirked an eyebrow at the words. Oh, yeah—because fifteen years was practically a whirlwind, wasn't it?

She lifted the hand that wasn't holding Evie and laid her

palm against his cheek, her thumb brushing against a hint of coarse stubble. 'Would you think less of me if I told you I could stand a little rushing?'

A purely sensual smile unfolded across his mouth. 'I think I'd like you more, actually.'

Colleen laughed softly.

So he leaned in and kissed her again. A slow kiss that spoke of things to come.

Colleen sighed contentedly when he lifted his mouth from hers. 'Yep, when I'm recovered it'll probably take me all of about ten minutes the first time. Just so you know.'

'Darlin'…' One large hand lifted her hand from his face to press a warm kiss into the palm. Then he fixed her with a heated gaze as he looked over the edge of her fingers. 'You'll have to trust me when I tell you that we're gonna take *way* more than ten minutes. I'm thinking hours, myself. Days, even. Once I start touching you I won't want to stop. And believe me when I tell you that I'd go into great detail about what I want to do to you if it weren't for young ears close by.'

If he couldn't see how she felt from the way she knew she was looking at him then she'd be stunned. Because sitting there with him, holding her baby and talking about making love together was quite possibly the most perfect moment she'd ever experienced.

For the first time in a very long time she felt anything was possible.

Eamonn was the love of her life after all. It might have been fate when she fell for him as a teenager. It might have been destiny that brought him back to her when she needed him most. Thing was, if it *were* those things then why shouldn't she try harder to let it happen?

Why was she fighting the things she wanted the most?

She had Evie, she had Eamonn talking about staying, about making love with her, and to top it off she still had Inisfree, even after everything that had happened.

What more did she really need?

So she laid it all on the line in a husky voice. 'I do trust that you don't want to hurt me. And I do want you. So much. I may not find it easy telling you these things, but it's not because they're not there, Eamonn. I need you to know that.'

The hold on her hand tightened. 'Yeah, I know.'

Colleen smiled across at him, her heart beating hard and loud against her breast. Maybe, just maybe, there was a possibility that happily ever after really could exist...

She almost allowed herself to believe that—until after she had finally put Evie down in her cot.

She hesitated in the hallway outside the nursery, her eyes falling on the light that arced from the open door of Eamonn's bedroom.

With a smile on her lips she padded towards it on her sock-covered feet, her approach muffled by the carpet. She might not be able to make love with him, but after the sheer beauty of their confessions in Evie's nursery she just wanted to be with him. To be held by him. To fall asleep in his arms and wake up beside him. To show some willingness to try, *really* try, to hold onto what they already had.

The smile grew as she got closer. His shadow was falling back and forth into the arc of light as he moved around his room.

It was just a shame she couldn't show him *properly*. After all, she had a world of fantasies to play out...

But when she got to the door and peeked around the edge she stopped dead. Staring wide-eyed at the sight of an open suitcase on his bed while he stood in front of it, folding trousers to pack them away.

And in that moment she had her heart stolen from her chest.

After everything he'd just said he was *leaving*? How could he *do* that? How could he get her to trust for the first time in a long time and then break it in less than a heartbeat?

It was just like the day she had found Adrian packing a bag. She had walked into the bedroom, in the Gatehouse she'd never been back to, and found him throwing things into a case. It had been the beginning of a downward spiral that had led her to the same thing all over again. This time to a man she loved with all of her soul, packing a suitcase to leave her.

Only this time the level of hurt was tenfold what it had been with Adrian. Because she'd never loved Adrian like she loved Eamonn—never wanted Adrian the way she ached for Eamonn. Adrian had never touched her soul and made her believe in happily ever after.

Even if that belief had only lasted for twenty minutes before dying a death.

'Early flight, *darlin'*?'

Eamonn froze. Closing his eyes for a moment, he swore softly before he turned round to look at her. 'I was going to tell you, but—'

One eyebrow quirked sarcastically as she interrupted him. 'But you thought you'd just have a go and see if I was ready for a little fun before you left?'

This time he swore loudly. 'I thought no such thing. I was going to tell you when I came upstairs, but when I saw you with Evie…'

His words trailed away. How did he even begin to tell her

what he'd felt as he'd stood in that doorway? There weren't words. Not words big enough anyway. And how could he even begin to explain to her when he still didn't have everything straight in his own mind?

While he hesitated, she folded her arms defensively across her breasts. And waited. A million accusations in her eyes.

It shocked Eamonn beyond belief. Surely she couldn't still think that he would leave and not come back? Not after everything that had happened between them?

Where had the feisty Colleen he'd fallen for gone to? The one who had been fighting tooth and nail to hang onto the place she loved so much? If she would just love him half as much as she loved Inisfree then nothing could pull them apart, could it? She'd fight for him then.

In a sad way, it was his parents all over again. One person who loved a place so much that they clung to it more than they did to another person they wanted to spend their life with. Surely lightning couldn't strike twice?

He fought his anger back as he dared a step closer to her. 'Don't look at me like that. For this to stand any chance of working you have to trust me.'

'How can I trust you if you don't talk to me? You're in here packing a damn bag before you've even told me you're going!' She unfolded her arms to wave a hand at the offending item. 'You'll be telling me next that you've already booked a flight and made the arrangements?'

Aw, hell. That was exactly what he'd done. But he hadn't done it to go behind her back or to make some kind of hasty getaway. He'd done it out of habit.

For half his life he'd been a man of action. When something needed to be done with any degree of urgency he stepped up to the plate, got the job done. It was only in his relationship with Colleen that he seemed capable of getting things so wrong without even trying.

Maybe simply because it was so important. Because he stood to lose so much of himself if it went wrong. Another example of how Colleen could knock him sideways. So that when he should have been getting things more right than he ever had, he just kept on messing up.

The fact she obviously had so little faith in him made him avoid answering her question directly, or admitting his mistake. 'There's a union strike. They need me to negotiate. I wouldn't be going if it wasn't important. But…' He stepped closer again, rationalising his actions. 'This contract we have with the city has a penalty clause if we come in late. If the strike isn't settled then we won't just have to pay that penalty, it'll affect the company's chances of further city tenders. It's a possible loss of millions of dollars' worth of work long-term. And I can't let that happen.'

But the full explanation he'd given to justify his leaving and to gloss over his mistake didn't have the calming effect he'd been aiming for. Instead her eyes widened and she took a step backwards.

'Millions of dollars? What do you mean, *millions* of dollars?' She searched his face. 'Just how successful *are* you in New York?'

He stood still. 'You said you'd followed my career.'

'Those articles didn't quote your bank balance!'

Eamonn sighed. 'Now you're going to use the fact I have money *against me*? Hell, Colleen, only *you* could do that.'

Her eyes flashed at him in warning. 'You let me talk about how you shouldn't have to spend money or invest in this place if it wouldn't work. I even worried about the damn expense of flying backwards and forwards between here and

the States. Not once did you correct me, or tell me you were
some kind of damn millionaire!'

'So you're mad at me because I didn't correct you? Or is
it because I didn't go wandering around wearing Armani and
throwing wads of cash at everyone? Tell me what it is that's
the biggest sin here—I'll hold my hand up for not telling you
quicker about leaving, but other than that I haven't done
anything wrong. Not twenty minutes ago you were telling me
you cared about me, that you wanted me. Are you now going
to tell me that that's changed because I have *money*? That
you'd be happier if I was a bum?'

She faltered. But, being Colleen, it wasn't for long. 'What
I'm telling you is that this is another example of how little I
know you. I really don't know you at all, *do I*? And how can
I know how I really feel if I don't know the real you?'

It wasn't just what she said that got to him. It was the look
in her eyes: a look of hurt, of disbelief. A look that said he'd
just tested her feelings for him and hadn't come out of it so
well.

Goddamn it. He hadn't done anything wrong! Why should
he have to justify it to her? Wasn't trying so hard to get her
to believe in them enough?

Eamonn shook his head. 'I don't know what to do, here.
I can't win with you.'

'It's not meant to be a competition.'

'No, it's meant to be a trust thing. A taking-a-chance-on-
something-that-could-be-incredible thing.' His heart was
thundering in his chest as his anger rose. He took one final
step her way to point a long finger at her. 'Don't you *dare*
judge me by what your ex did when he left you after making
promises he had no intention of keeping. I don't say things
if I don't mean them. So don't stand there and look for a ton

of reasons to justify pushing me away. Because that's *exactly* what you're doing, Colleen. And if I end up not coming back you'll have no one to blame but yourself.'

Her burst of laughter was sharply sarcastic, and reeked of bitterness. 'Running off into the sunset is what you do best, though, isn't it? It's history repeating itself, and it's only the players that have changed.'

It was a low blow. And suddenly Eamonn hadn't the energy to fight with her any more. Not when she could cause him actual physical pain with a few words. He could work through his own fears, and some of hers too—*if* she worked with him. But he couldn't do it alone.

Avoiding looking at the cold glint in her eyes, he glanced around the room before his eyes fell on his half-packed suitcase. He stepped away from her to continue packing.

'If there's one thing I've learnt about you these last few weeks it's that there's no talking to you when you dig your heels in. Not without badgering you, anyway. I don't have a choice about going, whether you choose to believe that or not. Maybe you should just have a think about what you want in the meantime.'

Out of his peripheral vision he saw that she stood in one place for a long time. So he concentrated on burying his anger at her lack of trust and continued to pack. Until he caught sight of her turning her back to him.

He left her with the one thing he wanted her not to forget. 'I believe you meant what you said in the nursery. You can't take it back now. And there may be things you don't know about me, just like there are things about you I don't know yet. But I want to learn. You just let me know if that's what you want too and I'll be here. I can't do much more than that.'

CHAPTER EIGHTEEN

MAYBE.

That was what she was reduced to again. A whole set of damn maybes. And they led her to wonder just when she had become so introverted, so defensive, so very *scared*. Had she let Adrian do that to her?

The very idea killed her. No way. Uh-uh. That man had taken enough from her. It wasn't him. Apart from guilt at having let him into her life in the first place, she had no feelings for him whatsoever.

Nope. All her present insecurities came from wanting something so very badly that she was afraid to reach out and take it. Big risks for big gains, the saying went. And it was so true.

Colleen McKenna wasn't that much of a coward, though. Was she? She hadn't used to be.

Maybe if she hadn't been transformed into a mother of late she would have been more prepared to take a risk. Having Evie made her more cautious, more wary. A mother's protective instinct at work. But then that meant she was hiding behind her daughter, just like Eamonn had said. And she couldn't do that either.

Evie deserved a happy mother. And without Eamonn

Colleen wasn't happy. It was just that simple. She knew that within hours of his leaving.

Maybe if she'd just taken the time to figure that out before he left. Maybe then she could have told him how very much she loved him, even if she didn't know him all that well yet. She knew what she needed to know.

Maybe, maybe, maybe.

Maybe if she hadn't got that phone call before she got to talk to him again.

'Inisfree Stud.'

'Hello, can I talk to Mr Eamonn Murphy, please?'

'I'm sorry, Eamonn had to go back to the States for a while. Can I take a message?'

'That would be great. It's Breige O'Connell from O'Connell and Dempsey, the auctioneers. I'm ringing about the enquiry he made about the valuation on the stud for sale…'

Colleen hadn't heard much after that. There had been something about how the woman had driven past and seen the improvements that had been made, and how that would add to the valuation, how she thought that doing the work had been a very wise investment. She'd even said 'speculate to accumulate', like Eamonn had. But Colleen had been too busy watching the world fall down around her ears.

When she'd put the phone down she had been dizzy. Then she'd had to run to be sick. Then Evie had woken up for a feed.

So she had fed her, rocking her in her arms while she wept silent tears. How could he? How *could* he?

For every single desperate explanation her heart found, her mind found a rational one in response. From the start—hell, before that, even—she had known that he would come back when Declan died. And had known part of that trip would be to settle his affairs so that he didn't have to come back again.

He had told her his trip could have lasted only a few days. Long enough to arrange the sale, her mind told her. Before he met you and saw you needed help, her heart responded. Then he saw what a mess the place was in and realised it would need work to make it a viable sale, her head said. But you told him why it was such a mess, and he hadn't the heart to tell you what he was going to do, her heart insisted.

Somewhere in there he started to genuinely care about you, her heart so dearly wanted her to believe.

Yeah, but then if that's true, what if he still wanted to sell the place to get you to go with him? her head asked her.

Eamonn had never loved Inisfree. Even if he genuinely cared about her, it didn't mean he'd automatically love the place now just because she did.

He was a millionaire property developer. A businessman at heart. Why on earth would he need a horse stud in some tiny corner of Ireland?

She'd never been so disappointed in someone. Not even Adrian. But then Adrian had never shared her legacy from birth. Adrian had never been the love of her life. Eamonn Murphy should have been so much more.

Well, he'd picked the wrong girl to play games with. If he knew her at all then he had to know she wouldn't let him sell Inisfree to the highest bidder. Even if it meant going to battle with the man she loved.

Seven hours on a plane, straight to the office, an update from Pete, shower and change, and then into the first negotiations with the union reps. No stopping.

Eamonn was running with the theory that the sooner he sorted everything out, the sooner he could get back to Colleen.

It was killing him, though.

Not just because he was so dog-tired. But because he found himself missing her presence with an ache that was a constant weight in his chest. So he wasn't nearly as sharp as he was renowned for being. And that slowed him down. Which, in turn, defeated his purpose of trying to keep going.

By the time his mind worked out that he'd screwed up the time differences it was too late to call her. And he cursed himself up and down for the mistake.

How was he supposed to keep convincing her he was serious if he couldn't make the time to call and reassure her? So he rang her the minute he woke up, his body still adjusting to the jet-lag. He got Lorna, the yard groom instead.

'She's not here.'

'Okay, will you tell her I'll call later?'

'No problem.'

Later he got the answer machine. 'Colleen, it's me. I tried earlier but you were out. I hope you and Evie are okay.' He hated talking to machines, but he needed to leave *something* that would let her know he hadn't quit on them. 'The negotiations aren't going so well, but I'll try to call you again in the next break. The sooner I can get this done the sooner I'll be back. So if I keep missing you when I call it's because I'm trying to get it done. I'll talk to you soon.'

In the next break he got the machine again. And it went on like that for days.

He was going slowly insane. And he was damn well going to get her mobile number when he *did* get to talk to her.

On the fourth day he set his alarm and slept for a while, waking in the early hours to make damn sure he caught her.

'Inisfree Stud.'

He smiled in relief at the sound of her voice. 'Hello, stranger.'

There was a hesitation, then, 'Hello.'

Even from thousands of miles away he could hear the chill in her voice. His smile faded. 'What's wrong?'

'Now, why would there be anything wrong?'

'I don't know. But there is. What is it?'

His attempt at keeping his voice soft did nothing to change her tone. 'Everything's just fine here. Don't worry. I'm finally getting things sorted out.'

Eamonn let out a breath he hadn't known he'd been holding. 'That's great. Is Evie missing me?'

'She's too little to miss you.'

'Well, how about you, then?'

Another hesitation. 'When do you think you'll get back?'

'As soon as I can.' He sighed. 'But at this rate it could be a couple of weeks. The union is—'

'Well, let me know. I have to go. Evie is awake, and one of the horses had colic last night so the vet is on his way.'

'Colleen, what's wrong?' This time his voice was firmer. 'Are you still mad because I didn't tell you I had to come back so soon?'

'No. I'm not mad because of that. I'm sure you didn't plan it. And you have work there. You had to go some time.'

She understood that? Well, that had to be a good sign. They were making progress after all. 'I'll be back as soon as I can.'

'Yes. Because you have unfinished business here, don't you?'

The honeyed tone to her voice had an immediate and visceral response from his body. And his voice dropped huskily in reply. 'You're damn right I do.'

'I have unfinished business with you too.'

'Well, then, I'll need to get these negotiations over and

done with so I can come over there and wrap that up.' He settled himself deeper into the cushions of his bed, his body reacting to the thought of a more intimate phone conversation about their 'unfinished business'.

'I'm surprised you just don't send me the paperwork and wrap it up from there. That would save you a flight back, wouldn't it?'

He scowled at the ceiling, his body stiffening in a different way as her angry words made their way down the line. So much for an intimate phone conversation. *'Now* what are you talking about? How in hell can I settle it from here? And *what* paperwork?'

'I had a nice phone call the day you left, from Breige O'Connell…'

'Who?' His exhausted mind searched frantically for a face to go with the name.

'One of the auctioneers you hired to sell this place.'

Oh, great. *That* Breige O'Connell. 'I talked to her before I even got over there to begin with.'

'My, aren't we organised?'

'I didn't call to have another argument with you.'

'Well, that's an awful shame, because that's what you're getting. And you'll sell Inisfree without my consent over my dead body. You hear me?'

'Now, wait just a minute—'

'No, I won't wait any minute. This place might not mean anything to you, Eamonn, but it's my home. And I won't let you sell it. It's just my luck to fall in love with someone too stupid to know that.'

Then the line went dead.

Eamonn threw the phone across the room, swearing loudly. He had never in all his born days met a woman who could make him so angry! If she'd waited that damn minute he could have told her that what he'd *planned* on doing when he went home was a world away from what he had ended up *wanting* when he got there. Yes, he'd wanted the place valued, so he'd know his figures when he approached her about selling her his share. All that had been was common sense. A practicality to be taken care of when he had nothing else left to do. There hadn't even been funeral arrangements to be made by the time he'd found out. And in his grief he had needed *something* to do.

But that had been before he'd got there. Before he'd met Colleen again. Before he'd known what she had been through and had been drawn to help her. Before he'd got to know her and been bowled over by her determination, her feisty temperament and her love for the place they'd both grown up in. Before her stubbornness had driven him to distraction and his attraction to her had sneaked up on him to tangle him in knots.

Before her child had been set into his arms and for the first time he had wanted to be entangled in the lives of others. Wanted something he'd never even thought he'd been looking for before.

He raked his hands through his hair and down over his face. She was so quick to doubt him, in such a hurry to think the worst of him. What was he doing, chasing after a woman so damned stubborn that she wouldn't take the time to talk to him and set things straight? Surely if she felt even a glimmer of what he felt she would want to try?

If he had half a head he would forget all about her and go right on living his life like he had before he—

Large hands stilled on his face. Then dropped down to his lap. *Hang on a minute.*

She'd just told him she loved him.

CHAPTER NINETEEN

OH, YEAH. This was what she'd missed. This sense of being alive, of being free, of having the rest of the world disappear in a blur around her as the wind blew against her face and hooves thundered on the ground beneath her.

While her horse galloped across the open countryside she could forget about everything else and focus only on being in harmony with the powerful animal. Her soul set free. And if she just concentrated on that feeling of exhilaration for long enough she could even try and pretend she was leaving her pain behind with every long stride.

Was it any wonder she loved these majestic animals when they were so much easier to be around than people?

On a horse's back she was in control, working with the animal to get the best results from each of them. And it raised a burst of joyous laughter from her as they approached the final hedge from home. She sat upright in the saddle, brought her legs in tighter against the horse's flanks, held the reins a little tighter to set her up for the jump.

And then she was in the air, flying for a moment before they landed safely on the other side. If she had to spend hours in the saddle every day to feel this way and temporarily forget her broken heart, then every horse on the yard was about to get fit. And fast.

But as she reined back into a canter, and then a trot, and finally a walk, Inisfree came back into sight at the bottom of the valley. And with the picture-perfect sight of it nestled in green fields on a sunny day came the ache.

That was what Eamonn had left her with. An ache so deep that every time she looked at the place she thought of him and the pain sliced her clean in two. So that seeing Inisfree wasn't the same any more. Because he wasn't there.

She hadn't heard a word from him since the last time they'd argued on the phone. When she'd blurted out how she felt in anger. And that hurt the most. That, after having accidentally given away how she felt about him, his response had been to disappear. To put a seal on her belief that he hadn't meant to stay in the first place.

It had all been a game to him. Another conquest to be made, to prove he could have what he wanted when he wanted it. And the fact that her deepest fears had been realised made her sorely want not to have loved him at all. Ever.

Because the Eamonn she had loved would never have done that to her. Not knowing what she'd already been through in the last year.

He'd made a lie of every thoughtful gesture, every spark of understanding, every warm smile and heated touch. So she was left wondering if she'd dreamt it all because her heart had wanted it so badly.

The horse twitched beneath her, dancing sideways as its head rose and ears pricked.

'All right, Meg. It's all right.' She leaned forwards and patted the mare's neck to soothe her as she glanced around to see what had caused her to get restless.

A horse's hearing being better than a human's over distance, it took a moment before she found the source. She recognised the horse straight away. Even if it hadn't been for the colour and size, she knew her own animals—and Bob's large form was hard to miss.

But it took being much closer before she recognised the rider. And her breath caught at the sight. *It couldn't be!*

But as Bob sedately cantered up the hill towards her she knew that it was. She might have recognised Eamonn's tall form sooner if she had seen him on a horse in the last twenty years.

Even while her traitorous heart beat louder in her chest she could feel her anger rising.

Just because Eamonn Murphy chose to finally ride towards her on a 'white charger', it didn't mean she was going to forgive him. It had been almost two long, torturous weeks since she'd hung up on him. And his getting on a horse after a couple of decades wasn't going to erase that kind of pain.

Calming Meg again as they got closer, she glared at him from the saddle. 'Suddenly remembered all your dad taught you, did you?'

Eamonn grinned at her from his saddle, obviously well pleased with himself. 'I took lessons because of you, as it happens. Two days at a school in New York. Right this minute I hurt in places I'm not even going to tell you about.'

'So you're John Wayne now?'

'Not quite.' He stroked a large hand along the wide neck. 'But Bob and I have an understanding—don't we, Bob?'

Colleen blinked at him in stark astonishment.

His eyes rose to meet hers, the gold sparkling at her across the divide as his voice dropped. 'If the mountain won't come to Mohammed…'

'You could have tried calling.'

That raised a bark of laughter. 'Yeah, because I love it when people hang up on me or don't take my calls.'

'Well, we'll never know what I would have done, will we?' She raised her chin and smiled sarcastically. 'Because you *didn't* call.'

'I had negotiations to get out of the way, and then a two-day wait for paperwork to be signed by all parties—which I filled with *riding lessons*. And, anyway, some things are better said in person.'

'Well, you could have saved yourself the trip.' She gathered the reins and legged Meg forward. 'There's nothing you have to say that I want to hear.'

'Oh, you might just be surprised.'

From the corner of her eye she saw him fall into step beside her and she sighed, tempted to urge her mare forwards and see just how much of his riding skills Eamonn remembered. It would serve him right if she aimed them at the nearest river. Bob *hated* water.

He glanced at her for a moment, then stared down the hill towards Inisfree. 'Okay, I'm just going to jump right in with all of this. Get it out of the way before another argument starts. Will you listen?'

'Why should I?'

'Because if you've been half as miserable as I have this last couple of weeks you'll want to try and clear this up. So will you listen? Or do I have to write it all down and send it through a neutral party? Like Evie.'

Colleen pursed her lips as she thought. The river was getting more attractive by the second. But he was right, *damn him*. She *had* been miserable. She was still miserable. But just because her traitorous heart was glad to see him, it didn't mean everything was resolved.

'You have as long as it takes to get to the yard, and then we're done.'

He sighed beside her—a sigh that spoke of frustration at her attitude. But, rather than argue with her again, he started talking in a calm, even tone. 'You're right. I *was* planning on selling the place. But that was before I came home again. I was planning on selling it to you, as it happens. But when I got here I knew straight away you couldn't afford it.'

'Well, I can afford it now. One of the sites has sold; the other one is under offer. And I'll sell another couple if I have to, to make up the difference after you get your share. So as soon as you're ready we'll talk figures.'

'I don't want to sell it. If you want to own it outright to remove any doubt between us, then fine: it's yours; I'll sign it over. But I don't want it on the open market. I never did. This is home. It always was.'

Colleen didn't answer. She'd had two long weeks to hate him for thinking about selling. Amongst other things. And, much as she hated to admit it to herself, the fact that he had made the effort to get on a plane, then get on a horse to come and explain it to her, meant something. As did his offer to sign the place over to her—not that she'd let him do that.

She would hear him out. She knew that. Wouldn't be able to stop herself from listening. But that was it. Now that she knew how much he could hurt her, she wasn't about to put herself through it again.

Eamonn's deep voice continued at her side. 'That's just the thing, you see. I haven't had another home since I left here. I've had a place to live, a place to work, made a few friends along the way. But it was never the same as having a place to call home.'

He was filling in the gaps. One of the things that had

made her stop and doubt what they had was the fact that she didn't really know him. The person he'd been in the time he'd been away. And now he was beginning to tell her, in a hypnotic, rumbling tone that softened the edges of her hardened heart. Even while she remained so determined to stay angry at him.

'A few years ago I got restless. I didn't know why. It wasn't like I wasn't successful. Or because I was lonely. At least I didn't think I was. But I guess I just needed something more than I had in my life.'

'Hence the trips to the Amazon, I suppose?' She risked a glance in his direction and he rewarded her with a smile that teased out his dimple.

'Haven't been there, as it happens. But, yes, hence the trips. I guess I was looking for something.' His eyes gleamed at her. 'It took me coming back here to find it. There's a certain irony in that, don't you think?'

Colleen *couldn't* think. Not in that instant. All she could do was stare at him while she took shuddering breaths. How could one person have such an immediate response from her just by looking at her? *Really?*

So he continued, breaking eye contact to look down the hill at their destination and taking a deep breath. 'When I said I didn't hate Inisfree, that wasn't entirely true. I *did* hate it for a while. When my mother left I blamed the place rather than the people. It was easier. If my father had loved her enough to give up the place he loved then she might have been around for longer. But as I got older I realised that the place didn't stop her from seeing me. She made that choice on her own. I don't think it was so much a case of her hating the place as hating what she had. She didn't want to be a wife and a mother, so it wouldn't have mattered where my dad chose to live. If she'd loved him that much then they'd have found a compromise. But they didn't even look for one. And that was their fault. Not the fault of Inisfree.'

Staring at his profile, Colleen knew that it was almost like history repeating itself. Except this time she was the one who had wanted to be a wife and a mother and to stay at Inisfree. It was Eamonn who had left.

Maybe there was as much of his mother in him as there was of his father? And yet he *had* tried to talk to her about a compromise, hadn't he? About meeting halfway to try and keep what they had.

And she'd shut him out. At every step. Doubting that her dream could ever be a reality.

Which she'd been right about. Because he'd still left. Even while a traitorous glimmer of hope started low in her chest she kept reminding herself of that as she listened to his steady tones and let the horses carry them in a slow walk down the field.

'Maybe when I left a part of me still hated the place. I thought I could do better, that maybe there was more of my mother's wanderlust in me than there was of my father's love for home and a steady foundation. I've always regretted that I wasn't mature enough to understand that I wasn't that different from him. It was my own sense of guilt at wanting to leave like she had that made me argue with him that day. I thought I could get more out of life than he had—that by staying I'd end up living a life he'd chosen for me rather than one I chose for myself. I wish that he could have been here today to see that the life I choose to have *is* here.' He fixed her with an intense gaze and her eyes locked with his. *'With you.'*

For a moment Colleen felt dizzy. Everything was fading out beyond the warmth in his eyes. And she was speechless, afraid that if she spoke she might break the spell, wake up from another dream.

His voice was huskier, deeper, as he took a chance and laid it all on the line. *'You're* my home, Colleen. Wherever you want to be, that's where I'll be. And you love this place, so that means I'll love it too. Because whatever makes you happy makes me happy. That's just the way it is.'

Her breathing sped up as the hope within her blossomed into a world of possibilities. Her heart was joyous with *I told you so's*. But her head still had a voice too. 'You can't give everything up for me because I want to live here. It's not fair. After time you'd hate me for it, and I can't let you to do that.'

'You could make a compromise with me, though. Meet me halfway, like I've been trying to ask you to, in a round-about way. We could prove that what we have is stronger than what my parents had by working together.'

She swallowed. 'How would we do that?'

Eamonn pulled on Bob's reins and waited until she'd swung Meg round so that they were side by side. 'I'll have to go back to New York fairly regularly. I told you that. Come with me whenever you can. And if there are times you can't, then always believe that I'll come home to you.'

'What about your travelling all over the place?'

He smiled softly. 'Well, somehow I don't think the need behind that exists any more. But everybody takes a holiday from time to time. So we'll take holidays. There are so many places I'd love you to see. Places that are special to me that I'll get to see all over again through your eyes. I think that would be pretty amazing.'

One by one he was working his way through all the things that had worried her. Like a checklist for happily ever after.

Could it be real? Could it be just that simple after all? That all it would need was a little risk-taking in the form of complete honesty?

Because, at the end of the day, putting your heart on the line was the biggest risk anyone ever took—wasn't it?

'What about Evie? I know she's not yours—'

'Now, you see, you're wrong there. She's been mine since the day I first held her. All she had to do was look at me with eyes the exact blue as yours and it was a done deal. And when she has a husband, and her own kids, she'll still be mine. If that's not how it feels to be a father then I don't know what is.'

Colleen's breath hitched in her chest, and she finally let go of her troublesome mind and trusted what her thudding heart was telling her. How could she not when he was saying all the things she needed to hear him say? When he had taken a chance on being rebuffed yet again by a woman who had pretty much done nothing *but* try to rebuff him every step of the way? If he was prepared to take so big a chance, to come all this way to convince her of his sincerity, how could she turn him away again?

It was what she wanted, after all.

Steering Meg a step closer, she smiled at Eamonn with shimmering eyes.

He reached out and took one of her hands off the reins, twining his fingers with hers. 'Just in case you haven't got it already, Colleen McKenna, I'm in love with you. It took a while for me to understand what it was I felt. But that night I looked in on you and Evie in the nursery I knew that my whole world was in that room. I've spent years chasing about all over the planet, when all I could ever want was waiting for me here. You are the most infuriatingly stubborn, feisty, brave, beautiful woman I've ever met. I could spend the rest of my life searching and I'll never find another woman like you.'

Tears were welling in her eyes, and Colleen let them fall without hiding them. She didn't have to hide anything any more. 'I loved you when I was fifteen, just so you know. You broke my heart when you left. This last while I think all I've done is fill in time 'til you came back. It was only when I lost hope and let my doubts take over that I made a mess. Because I wasn't brave enough to hope for a happily ever after—not after all that's happened.'

Eamonn grinned and squeezed her fingers tight. 'Well, it's here now. For both of us. If you'll let it be.'

'Yes.' She squeezed his fingers back. 'I love you so much.'

'I know you love me.' He grinned over at her. 'You told me on the phone.'

Colleen laughed—a joyous laugh that was echoed by Eamonn. 'I didn't mean to say it, and I wasn't sure you'd heard me. Because if you had, and you'd felt the same, you'd have *called* me!'

He shook his head. 'And miss all this romance?'

'Well…' She nodded with a mischievous sparkle in her eyes. 'Everything's better when there are horses around.'

'If you love me half as much as these flipping animals then we'll do just fine, you and me.'

'I do. Ten times more.'

'*Wow*. Now I *know* it's true.' He tried to lean forwards, but Bob chose that moment to move and he laughed again. 'If you love me, you'll tell me how to keep this beast still so I can kiss you!'

She smiled, waited a single heartbeat, and then demanded in a steady voice, 'Bob. *Stand*.'

Bob did as he was told, and they leaned closer. Inches

from her mouth, Eamonn smiled a sensual smile, the gold in his eyes radiating heat. 'If you're on a horse, then I take it you're feeling better?'

Both reins still held in one hand, she freed her fingers from his and threaded them through the dark curls at the nape of his neck, her voice dropping seductively. 'I had my six-week check-up, and apparently I'm in *very* good order. That'll be all the horse-riding over the years.'

Eamonn groaned. '*Thank you*, horses. I may learn to love them just for that alone.' He moved closer, his mouth hovering over hers. 'Mind you, maybe we should wait 'til the honeymoon. Seeing we've waited this long.'

Colleen laughed a low, husky, purely sexual laugh, her hand drawing his head down. 'Speak for yourself. I've already waited fifteen years.'

His mouth descended on hers, and he kissed her with weeks' worth of longing and years' worth of promises. And Colleen kissed him back, without any reservations, not coming up for air until her pulse was beating rapidly in her veins and her body was heated to boiling point.

Then she smiled at him, her heart in her eyes. 'Welcome home, Eamonn.'

0107 Gen Std HB

MILLS & BOON®

Live the emotion

FEBRUARY 2007 HARDBACK TITLES

ROMANCE™

The Marriage Possession *Helen Bianchin*   978 0 263 19572 9
The Sheikh's Unwilling Wife *Sharon Kendrick* 978 0 263 19573 6
The Italian's Inexperienced Mistress *Lynne Graham*
    978 0 263 19574 3
The Sicilian's Virgin Bride *Sarah Morgan*   978 0 263 19575 0
The Rich Man's Bride *Catherine George*   978 0 263 19576 7
Wife by Contract, Mistress by Demand *Carole Mortimer*
    978 0 263 19577 4
Wife by Approval *Lee Wilkinson*   978 0 263 19578 1
The Sheikh's Ransomed Bride *Annie West*   978 0 263 19579 8
Raising the Rancher's Family *Patricia Thayer* 978 0 263 19580 4
Matrimony with His Majesty *Rebecca Winters* 978 0 263 19581 1
In the Heart of the Outback... *Barbara Hannay* 978 0 263 19582 8
Rescued: Mother-To-Be *Trish Wylie*   978 0 263 19583 5
The Sheikh's Reluctant Bride *Teresa Southwick*
    978 0 263 19584 2
Marriage for Baby *Melissa McClone*   978 0 263 19585 9
City Doctor, Country Bride *Abigail Gordon*   978 0 263 19586 6
The Emergency Doctor's Daughter *Lucy Clark* 978 0 263 19587 3

HISTORICAL ROMANCE™

A Most Unconventional Courtship *Louise Allen* 978 0 263 19751 8
A Worthy Gentleman *Anne Herries*   978 0 263 19752 5
Sold and Seduced *Michelle Styles*   978 0 263 19753 2

MEDICAL ROMANCE™

His Very Own Wife and Child *Caroline Anderson*
    978 0 263 19788 4
The Consultant's New-Found Family *Kate Hardy*
    978 0 263 19789 1
A Child to Care For *Dianne Drake*   978 0 263 19790 7
His Pregnant Nurse *Laura Iding*   978 0 263 19791 4

MILLS & BOON®

0107 Gen Std LP

Live the emotion

FEBRUARY 2007 LARGE PRINT TITLES

ROMANCE™

Purchased by the Billionaire *Helen Bianchin*	978 0 263 19423 4
Master of Pleasure *Penny Jordan*	978 0 263 19424 1
The Sultan's Virgin Bride *Sarah Morgan*	978 0 263 19425 8
Wanted: Mistress and Mother *Carol Marinelli*	978 0 263 19426 5
Promise of a Family *Jessica Steele*	978 0 263 19427 2
Wanted: Outback Wife *Ally Blake*	978 0 263 19428 9
Business Arrangement Bride *Jessica Hart*	978 0 263 19429 6
Long-Lost Father *Melissa James*	978 0 263 19430 2

HISTORICAL ROMANCE™

Mistaken Mistress *Margaret McPhee*	978 0 263 19382 4
The Inconvenient Duchess *Christine Merrill*	978 0 263 19383 1
Falcon's Desire *Denise Lynn*	978 0 263 19384 8

MEDICAL ROMANCE™

The Sicilian Doctor's Proposal *Sarah Morgan*	978 0 263 19335 0
The Firefighter's Fiancé *Kate Hardy*	978 0 263 19336 7
Emergency Baby *Alison Roberts*	978 0 263 19337 4
In His Special Care *Lucy Clark*	978 0 263 19338 1
Bride at Bay Hospital *Meredith Webber*	978 0 263 19533 0
The Flight Doctor's Engagement *Laura Iding*	978 0 263 19534 7

0207 Gen Std HB

MILLS & BOON®

Live the emotion

MARCH 2007 HARDBACK TITLES

ROMANCE™

The Billionaire's Scandalous Marriage *Emma Darcy*
978 0 263 19588 0

The Desert King's Virgin Bride *Sharon Kendrick*
978 0 263 19589 7

Aristides' Convenient Wife *Jacqueline Baird*   978 0 263 19590 3

The Pregnancy Affair *Anne Mather*   978 0 263 19591 0

Bought for Her Baby *Melanie Milburne*   978 0 263 19592 7

The Australian's Housekeeper Bride *Lindsay Armstrong*
978 0 263 19593 4

The Brazilian's Blackmail Bargain *Abby Green*   978 0 263 19594 1

The Greek Millionaire's Mistress *Catherine Spencer*
978 0 263 19595 8

The Sheriff's Pregnant Wife *Patricia Thayer*   978 0 263 19596 5

The Prince's Outback Bride *Marion Lennox*   978 0 263 19597 2

The Secret Life of Lady Gabriella *Liz Fielding*   978 0 263 19598 9

Back to Mr & Mrs *Shirley Jump*   978 0 263 19599 6

Memo: Marry Me? *Jennie Adams*   978 0 263 19600 9

Hired by the Cowboy *Donna Alward*   978 0 263 19601 6

Dr Constantine's Bride *Jennifer Taylor*   978 0 263 19602 3

Emergency at Riverside Hospital *Joanna Neil*   978 0 263 19603 0

HISTORICAL ROMANCE™

The Wicked Earl *Margaret McPhee*   978 0 263 19754 9

Working Man, Society Bride *Mary Nichols*   978 0 263 19755 6

Traitor or Temptress *Helen Dickson*   978 0 263 19756 3

MEDICAL ROMANCE™

A Bride for Glenmore *Sarah Morgan*   978 0 263 19792 1

A Marriage Meant To Be *Josie Metcalfe*   978 0 263 19793 8

His Runaway Nurse *Meredith Webber*   978 0 263 19794 5

The Rescue Doctor's Baby Miracle *Dianne Drake*
978 0 263 19795 2

0207 Gen Std LP

Live the emotion

MARCH 2007 LARGE PRINT TITLES

ROMANCE™

HISTORICAL ROMANCE™

MEDICAL ROMANCE™